BETSEY BROWN

BOOKS BY NTOZAKE SHANGE

for colored girls who have considered suicide/when the rainbow is enuf

nappy edges

Three Pieces

Spell #7

A Photograph: Lovers in Motion

Boogie Woogie Landscapes

Sassafrass, Cypress & Indigo

A Daughter's Geography

From Okra to Greens

Some Men

Melissa & Smith

See No Evil

Ntozake Shange

BETSEY BROWN

A N O V E L

ST. MARTIN'S PRESS
NEW YORK

All the characters, places, and events in this story are fictional. Resemblance to real people or places is coincidence.

For information, address St. Martin's Press,
175 Fifth Avenue, New York, N.Y. 10010

Design by Janet Tingey

Library of Congress Cataloging in Publication Data
Shange, Ntozake.
Betsey Brown.
1. Title.
PS3569.H3324B4 1985 813'.54 85-2663
ISBN 0-312-07727-0
ISBN 0-312-07728-9 (pbk.)

Many thanks to all those involved in the ten-year saga of *Betsey Brown,* the novel, especially Ifa, Bisa, Paul, and my parents, as well as the annual encouragement of Joseph Papp, Bonnie Daniels, and my editor, Michael Denneny. As Jessica says, "We'll show you some real rock & roll" or as Olga says, "We let the pot steep till the kettle was black." It takes all that to make a little girl herself.

This book is dedicated to my family.

& this is for the man who chases butterflies
& alcoholics in latin night club dreams
& kisses me with zoom lenses on the beaches
of the Hollywood Freeway
all the hibiscus bloom as you devour iguanas
& this is for the men who loved me &
the one I love
& the child who is a mirror

—Jessica Hagedorn
"Something About You"
Dangerous Music, Momo's Press

BETSEY BROWN

ONE

The sun hovered behind a pink haze that engulfed all of St. Louis that Indian summer of 1959. The sun was a singular preoccupation with Betsey. She rose with it at least once a week. She'd shake Sharon or Margot outta they beds and run to the back porch on the second floor to watch the horizon set a soft blaze to the city. Their house allowed for innumerable perspectives of the sun. From the terrace off Betsey's room, where she was not 'sposed to stand, she could see the sun catty-cornered over the Victorian houses that dotted the street, behind maples and oaks grown way over the roofs of the sleeping families. On her street you could name the families without children in one breath. Why, one reason to live there was cause there were so many children. Only the Blackmans directly cross from Betsey with their pillars and potted dwarf plants didn't like children, which must be why they didn't have any. In the wintertime Mrs. Blackman would come running out in her furs, shouting for everybody to get off her lawn, even though it was the best one for sledding cause there were two slopes. Whatta shame she couldn't understand that. Yet seen from the terrace, when the dawn came in the winter, Mrs. Blackman's dwarfed plants wrapped in shields of ice glistened like rainbows. Betsey never told Mrs. Blackman that. She didn't mention the shadows of the nuns dressing in the convents, either. There was a preciousness to St. Louis at dawn or dusk that was settling to the child in the midst of a city that rankled with poverty, meanness, and shootings Betsey was only vaguely aware of.

The sun and the stairways protected her, gave her a freedom that was short-lived but never failing. Her house sat on a small hill and there were stairs that went to the front door, but you could use the same stairs to go anywhere around the house cause the stairs also led to a porch that went all the way round the side of the house. That's how come nobody could ever tell exactly where Grandma was. She could be anywhere on that porch just watching you do wrong. Then there were the back stairs, only three of them: one, two, three wooden ones, all creaky and needing paint. Underneath those stairs Betsey helped a stray cat have babies. She lined up worms and rocks. She lay flat on her back sometimes, being quiet and unseen, while everybody went looking for her or while everybody was coming up the steps. She heard a lot of secrets lying under the back stairs. Heard a lot of kissing. Now, kissing is hard to hear, but Charlie kissed back there sometimes. Jane and Greer were always kissing. The stairs to the basement were magnificently narrow, like a dungeon the basement was. In the summer it was ever so cool and in the winter it was warm. Betsey didn't know why more of the family didn't covet the basement. Maybe it was on account of the dark and the smell. It smelled funny down there. Jane said that white folks usedta make the colored help sleep down there. Now that Jane would never do, put a Negro in the basement.

But the best stairs were the back stairs that went all the way to the third floor. These stairs turned this way and then that. Why, a body would hide in a cranny on those stairs and never be found. They were dark, too, a blackish wood gainst blackish walls like servants should never see the light of day. Betsey loved the back stairs that led to the littlest porch on the third floor, which Jane never warned her about, cause Jane'd never seen it, Betsey 'sposed. From there, on fall mornings, in her pajamas and overcoat, Betsey watched the dawn come up over the steeple of the church way down Union Boulevard, past Soldan and the YMHA. The bells would cling a holy cling that no one in the house could hear. They used alarm clocks.

So Betsey had fashioned parameters of her own for the house she shared with everyone else. The only real problem was doors. Every room was connected to another room by a door and Jane forbade anyone to lock the doors. The second floor was a pathway of bedrooms with a hallway right next to it. Only Charlie's room wasn't connected to anything and that was because he was in high school. Betsey didn't see what kinda reason that was to have a room that wasn't connected to everybody else's. That's why Betsey liked to be up before everyone else, out on one of her porches, taking in the world all on her own. There she made up stories or just stayed out of the fracas Sharon, Margot, and Allard would be making all the time. Sound traveled uncannily in this house and everybody was always yelling to everybody else. Arguing all the time. Howdy-Doody or American Bandstand, Little Rock or Amos and Andy.

Alone on her balcony, Betsey luxuriated in the quietness, letting her thoughts ramble.

"Speak up Ike, an' 'spress yo'se'f," Betsey murmured, remembering yesterday afternoon on Union Boulevard when Willetta and Susan Ann had ripped into each other over that basketball champ with the good hair, Benny. Betsey kept trying to remember how Willetta's bra looked and how Susan Ann had scratched Willetta's face with the longest red nails. She was certain that the black-laced bra and the red nails had something to do with the way Mr. Paul Laurence Dunbar wanted her to say, "Speak up Ike, an' 'spress yo'self." Some sultry willing-to-fight-over-you,-if-you-give-me-a-chance way of saying the line. Today Mrs. Mitchell was having the elocution contest for Class 7B, Betsey's class, with the kids from cross the tracks and the kids from the right side of em too. Willetta and Susan Ann had gathered such a crowd round em, tearing at each other that way. And Benny, he just went on to the game gainst Sumner, like he didn't know nothin bout all this blood and swearing and cussing going on in his name. It was evil and wicked to fight, but Betsey wanted the grown woman bit of it to rub off on her today when she said, "Speak up Ike, an' 'spress yo'self."

"I told you, you had to be out of the bathroom in five minutes! What do you think I'm gonna do? Go to school stink on accounta you take so long, Margot," Sharon was screaming round the corner from Betsey's room. How could she become a great anything with all this foolishness going on around her?

"Listen here, heifer. I'm gonna be in that bathroom in three minutes or you never gonna play with my jacks and I'ma tell Jeannie not to speak to you ever again. Do you hear me? Do you *hear* me?"

Sharon was kicking the bathroom door with her saddles making black streaks long the side board when Jane rolled over in her bed to touch Greer, just once more before her hellish day began. Where was Betsey with her coffee? Why was Sharon shouting the devil out in the hall? How could all this be happening to her?

"Sharon, I am going to whip you good, if I hear you call your sister or anybody else a heifer. Do you hear me? Just wait your turn. The boys are finished and you'll have plenty of time." Jane managed to raise her voice, if not her body. Something had to be done with all these children. "Greer, please, let's not have any more children. But can we make a little bitty bit of love?" Jane was tustled in a mass of auburn hair. Somehow her lavender nightgown was entwined in her arms beneath the pillows. She rolled toward her husband, who, as always when in a good mood, grabbed her reddish ringlets and pulled her mouth to his. The answer was yes, a long and sweet yes.

"Betsey, Betsey, where's my coffee?" Jane breathed deep

longing for more of her Greer and that caffeine. She could smell the coffee perking downstairs which meant that Mama was up and about, making lunches for all the children. "Betsey, where is my coffee?" Greer nuzzled a little closer and Jane simmered down and was all purr and open. She forgot about coffee.

Betsey wasn't even dressed, and she hadn't gotten her mama's coffee or her lines right yet. She ran like the Holy Ghost down the back stairs to set up Jane's cup and saucer before Grandma had to do it and broke something. "Speak up Ike, an' 'spress yo'self" rambling through her mind, her little girl hips twitched the way she imagined Susan Ann's had after she left Willetta in the street with nothing but her panties on. Not even a ponytail clasp was on that child once Susan Ann was done. Grandma sure enough had the coffee done.

"Seems to me a child could make an effort to take her hardworking mother a teeny ol' cup of coffee," Grandma murmured in her Carolinian drawl. There was a way about Vida that was so lilting yet direct that Betsey sometimes thought her grandma had a bloodline connection to Scarlett O'Hara.

"I'm sorry, Grandma, but I was practicing my elocution."

"You should have practiced your elocution last evening, instead of jumping all that colored double roping with those trashy gals from round the way."

Grandma poured her daughter's coffee, knowing full well what was goin on upstairs. Her daughter didn't have no common sense, that was the problem. Awready there was a house fulla chirren and she wouldn't stop messin' with that Greer. Jane was lucky, Grandma thought. None of the chirren looked like him, all dark and kinky-headed. Now it was true that

Betsey had a full mouth. Margot was chocolate brown. Sharon had a head fulla nappy hair. Allard was on the flat-nosed side. But in Grandma's mind Jane had been blessed, cause each of the chirren was sprightly and handsome on a Geechee scale, not them island ones but the Charlestonians who'd been light or white since slavery. But Grandma didn't like to think bout slavery. She was most white. Slaves and alla that had nothing to do with her family, until Jane insisted on bringing this Greer into the family and he kept making family. Lord knows who could help her.

"Here, Betsey, you carry this on up to your mama, and tell her I said that Allard needs to be looked at for the ringworm and Charlie needs a whipping for calling Sharon out of her name and all the lunches are packed, but I do feel a mite weak and need to rest my bones. I do wish she would quit that old job social-workering and mind you chirren more. I surely do."

Betsey took the coffee from Grandma ever so carefully. She was running late. Her teeth weren't even brushed yet and Charlie was in the bathroom for the second time. Mama still didn't have her coffee, and wouldn't have it when she imagined, cause Betsey drank the whole cup by the time she reached the top of the back stairs that twisted this way and that, leaving a girl time to dream of things to come and womanish ways.

When Betsey reached the top of the winding stairs with the empty cup, she quickly swallowed the little bit that had dropped into the saucer and with military precision made an about face, balancing her mother's wedding china in one hand, feigning a fan in the other, whispering, "Speak up Ike, 'spress yo'self." She could hear Charlie and Sharon arguing about how long was the circumference of the world. Margot adding, "As big as your head." Betsey almost dropped the delicate flowered cup rimmed with gold, seemingly atop a throne of its own. Jane was strolling down the hall, shouting the other way, "Betsey, where's my coffee?"

Sharon was trying to comb Margot's head a hair with a brush that looked like it was only big enough for Betsy Wetsy. "I can't help it. It's the only one I could find." Margot was tying Allard's shoes as he looked around the ceilings for shadows where the spooks that swept down on him in his dreams must live. "I know they're up there, Sharon. Let's getta broom and beat em to the death. Okay?" Sharon had Margot making faces verging on distortion; that hair, that hair had to be combed or Mama was gonna have a fit. "Well, we could tie it with a shoestring in a ponytail," Sharon conceded. Margot smiled so much she cried one big tear. Allard kept trying to get their attention: "Listen, if you all don't help me beat out them spooks, I'm gonna burn em up."

Together Sharon and Margot shouted, "Allard, keep your hands off them matches, do you hear?" Jane heard. Greer was apparently downstairs, already strains of Charlie Parker wafted through the house. Jane was powdering herself by her vanity in a gleam of nostalgia by her wedding photo. Oh that day had been so perfect, so soft and white. Whatta night they had at the Savoy. Why, she danced until she most fainted. Jane giggled and then regained her more official "mother's" stance as Betsey entered the room.

"Well, Betsey, I thought you must have gone all the way to Guatemala to get my coffee."

"No, Mommy, I just was practicing my elocution, when the

kids were making all this noise and you wanted your coffee and Grandma insisted on telling me how lucky we look the way we look because of Daddy. There was an awful lot goin on, Mama, honest."

Jane smiled at her miracle child. The baby she thought she couldn't have. What an error of judgment that had been. Still and all, Betsey was her first baby and close to her heart in a peculiar way, as if some real part of her walked out the door every time Betsey went down the front stairs or leaned gossiping, girl-like, over the back porch. Jane pulled Betsey to her, then took a few sips of coffee made exactly how she liked, milk in first, two sugars. And plenty of coffee. Jane still insisted on having her good china and cloth napkins for her coffee upstairs. "There's no reason to give up everything gracious on account of a few moments of hardship" was what she always said if Betsey brought a paper napkin or a mug to her room.

"Mama, you wanna listen to a little bit of my elocution preparation? I'm doing Mr. Paul Laurence Dunbar."

Jane thought, taking her time mischievously, and then shook her head yes.

"Betsey, of course I want to hear your interpretation of Dunbar, but hurry. You know your daddy's getting the morning quiz ready."

Betsey ran to her mama's closet and grabbed the first red womany thing she saw, a scarlet slip she draped round her hips. Jane's eyebrows rose, but she contained herself. After all, elocution was close to theater. Betsey stationed herself by her mother in front of the vanity, wanting to watch her every gesture and facial expression. Mama knew this poem awready, so she had to be good, or at least that's what she thought.

Jane thought anything her little girl did was just fine, but it pleased her that Betsey wanted to impress her.

"Who dat knockin' at de do'?
Why, Ike Johnson, yes, fu' sho!
Come in, Ike. I's mighty glad
You come down. I t'ought you's
mad
At me 'bout de othah night,
An was stayin' 'way fu' spite.
Say, now, was you mad fu' true
W'en I kin' o' laughed at you?
Speak up, Ike, an 'spress yo'se'f."

Betsey sashayed and threw her teeny hips, glinted her eyes, and coyly demonstrated her newly learned skills as coquette, much to her mother's delight. Jane hugged her girl and was about to offer some dramatic advice, when the morning rituals, authorized and unauthorized, overshadowed them and interrupted that very special moment they'd shared.

"Who's got my geography book?"

"Come on, tie my shoes."

"That dress is not yours. Give it here."

"Lord, Lord, please help me with these chirren."

"I'ma tell Daddy you took my books."

"I bet you won't have no backside side, if he gets holdt to ya."

"Come tie my shoes, please."

"For God's sake, somebody tie Allard's shoes."

"Margot, you better do something with that mess you call hair."

"You said you would comb it for me."

"She sure 'nough did."

"Where's my geography book?"

"Somebody tie Allard's shoes, fore he trips over himself."

"I'ma tell Daddy." The refrain arose from everyone's lips.

No one could find Allard to tie his shoes. Meanwhile Greer had strapped his conga drum round his shoulder. It was the one he'd brought from Cuba where Sharon was conceived under a sky of shooting stars, or so the story went. As if he were a southern Mongo Santamaria, Greer mamboed up the back stairs, through the halls, and down the front steps, gathering the mass of family he called his own, chanting all the while.

"The Negro race is a mighty one
The work of the Negro is never done
Muscle, brains, and courage galore
Negroes in this house
Meet me at the back door
Oh! the Negro race is a mighty one
Each and every one of you is an example of one
Oh! the Negro race is a mighty one
We goin to show the world
What can be done
Cause the Negro race is a mighty one."

Jane was not crazy about her children screaming at each other or about her husband's idea of reveille. Cuba, yes. St. Louis, no. St. Louis was still an old-fashioned place. With "Yes, M'ams" and "No, Sirs" grating Jane's ears every time she heard one of her children say sucha thing, but Greer swore it wouldn't hurt them and Greer knew a lot about the worlds Jane had never considered. Matisse, Gauguin, Pippin, Bearden, and Modigliani. Whenever Dizzy Gillespie came to town, there they were, justa waiting. If Chuck Berry was in a scrap with the law, there they were. Greer operating and Jane taking pictures. Sometimes she couldn't believe what she did for this man. Love and buckshot, music and street diagnoses, late-night feuds bout the future of the Negro race, whether DuBois or Walter White hadda place and where. That time DuBois had carried Betsey to bed was history. Everybody knew what a crotchety ol' figure of a man he was, but couldn't nobody but W.E.B. himself get that child to sleep. Was like the night Betsey'd hid in the back seat of the car to see Tina Turner, as if nobody would want to collect a ticket from her or see some I.D. from an eleven-year-old at the bawdiest night spot on the wrong side of the tracks. Saying "I wanna be an Ikette" didn't do it. Greer had to hightail it back to the house with his girl, trying to explain that Tina Turner didn't accept applications from young women under the age of eighteen. From that second, Betsey decided she would do everything just like Tina Turner do. Greer knew that and that worried him, and then again, he was assured Betsey'd be good at whatever she put her mind on.

Why couldn't Greer see what kind of an influence he was having on the children, Jane worried. Her sister would never have let Charlie stay with them if she'd known all this was going on.

Betsey'd run off behind her father to get ready for the morning quiz. Up and down and round about the house they went with Greer chanting, the children dancing.

They all marched into the kitchen where Grandma sat in a corner by the window that opened on an oak tree frequented by bluejays she fed whenever something was simply beyond her. She hummed, "I been 'buked, & I been scorned." Her daughter had married a mad man, bringing all this Africa mess into her house. Low-down music and prize-fighters at his heels soon as he stepped through the door. Nothing but the lowest of the low appealed to him, cept for her daughter, Jane. How could this be going on in her family? What would her father have thought in his starched trolley-driving uniform? What would her poor early-passt-on mother have made of a household run in such a brazen manner?

Greer paraded the children in file past Grandma to get their lunches and the 35¢ he left in stacks for each of them. Then he began.

"Betsey, what's the most standard of blues forms?"

"Twelve-bar blues, Daddy."

"Charlie, who invented the banjo?"

"Africans who called it a banjar, Uncle Greer."

"Sharon, what is the name of the President of Ghana?"

"Um . . . Nkrumah, I think."

"Thinking's not good enough, a Negro has got to know. Besides, it's Kwame Nkrumah. Margot, where is Trinidad?"

"Off the coast of Venezuela, but it's English-speaking."

"Allard."

Everybody turned around, realizing that Allard was nowhere to be seen. Grandma tutted to herself in the corner. At least one of the chirren wasn't taken in by this mess. Yet if Allard was missing, he was up to something terrible. That boy just loved fires.

"Allard!" Greer shouted out to the back porch, "Allard, come in this minute and put those matches down."

Allard let loose of the rags he'd been piling up and ran back to the house just before his father's hand would have laid a whap, lickety-split.

"Allard, you and I are going to have a talk this evening, but right now I want to know what discipline is?"

Discipline? All the children looked at each other askance. Daddy never asked questions like that. He asked fun questions about the Negroes, or music, or foreign places where colored people ran countries all their own and on their own. "What is discipline?" Now, that wasn't Daddy's kinda question at all.

Allard looked up ingenuously at his father with his shoes still untied, making little lakes around his legs, and answered: "Discipline is the hallmark of a mighty people." Then he sat down to try to tie his shoes again.

When Jane entered the kitchen, the line of children melted into hugs and kisses good-bye to Grandma and thanks to Daddy for the extra nickel for correctly answered questions at morning drill. No one bothered to figure where Allard got his answer from, but it must have been right cause Greer gave him five copper pennies. Jane had found time to do her nails, her hair and face, so she looked more like she was going shopping at Saks than to the segregated colored hospital to work with the crazy ones, the mad niggahs couldn't nobody else talk to. Betsey's word had been "psychopath" one time and she answered, "Mama's patients, niggahs what aint got no sense," for which she'd been sent to her room. Jane was furious. Of all of her children, Betsey should have understood it wasn't that folks didn't have any sense, it was that they were in pain and had so little, so very little to look forward to. Jane loved to miss the morning drill, and show up just in time for a grin from each urchin, a tidying of heads and belts, a moment to take pride in her womb's work. Every time she turned around she was poking out again. Jane loved being pregnant and she loved her children. She loved Greer, motioning for her to get a move on.

"Betsey, good luck today. Allard and Charlie, don't play too rough. Sharon, I bet you get at least a ninety on your geography test. Margot, those are lovely ponytails you've made for yourself. Mama, see you later. Enjoy the TV and let me know what is going on on 'Edge of Night,' you hear."

Greer chimed in, "That's right, Mama, take it easy and I'll bring you something nice. You mustn't strain yourself on accounta your heart. Take a stroll before the heat's too much. I'm gonna bring you something nice."

Jane and Greer sauntered to the car like young lovers. The children raced out the screen door, slammin it each time. "See ya, Grandma," "Bye-bye," "Back after basketball," "Love you, Grandma."

Only Betsey lingered on the porch next to the forsythia and azalea that Grandma loved so much. "Speak up, Ike, an' 'spress yo'se'f." The gentle old lady moved from her bluejays and robins toward her sweet child saying, "It's a matter of faith, Betsey, alla matter of faith." Betsey looked up at her grandma and took a deep breath, those southern eyes were sure of her. Her grandma's silken hands twisted her bangs a bit to the left.

"Betsey, if your grandpa could see you today I swear he'd be so proud. One of his own reciting from the great Mr. Dunbar. Yes, my Frank would certainly have loved to hear your very own rendition in that dialect of our times. I wisht you coulda seen him. I'ma pray for you, ya hear."

With that, Grandma grabbed up her apron and sat upon the porch glider to let the morning sun in her soul as she watched Betsey meander down the driveway with a sullen grace and a child's pace. Then Betsey stood absolutely still, shouting at the top of her lungs "SPEAK UP, IKE, I'S MIGHTY GLAD TO SEE YOU," and off she ran.

From the back porch Grandma could see only the carefully tended beds of tulips and the lengths of coral roses that Mr. Jeff looked after for the family. The small play yard that this ragamuffin loafer had erected for the children when they were little was now the gathering place for Betsey's imaginary friends, her digs to China, and the ripest honeysuckle vines to be found north of Charleston, or so it seemed to Vida. The quiet of the breeze and the smells of roses, honey, and her fresh cornbread eased her soul. Whenever she thought on Jane and that Greer her heart would getta fluttering and she'd verge on shortness of breath. Caint live nobody's life for em, but sometimes Vida wisht to the Heavens she could get inside her daughter's skin and find out how she got in this predicament. The stories were gonna come on and she was gonna remember to tell Jane bout "Edge of Life," or was it "Edge of Night"? Her memory wasn't what it usedta be, couldn't even crochet anymore cause she'd forget what she was making and for who. But it didn't cause anybody any fretting, Grandma was the gem of the household, fulla more stories than a bunch of Will Rogers could ever have told.

Mostly she talked on Frank, her long-passt-on husband, the Valentino of Allendale and the hills there'bout. He was sucha gentle man and couldn't nobody tell he was a Negro, not even when he opened his mouth. Fine diction, mighty fine articulation, Vida'd recall. His dark hair hangin like a drop of black honey cross his eye; that part as straight as a Cherokee's aim. Yes, her Frank was a truly fine man. Not on the order of the modern men of color she'd come across in her daughter's life. No, there was a gentleness bout Frank that they'd lost. Maybe it was the war. No, it couldn't be, Frank had served in '17 in Germany.

"Take it easy and I'll bring you something nice," that's what that Greer had said, as if presents could make up for how black and kinky-headed he was. Oh now, she mustn't think like that. After all he'd done for Jane. What all he'd done to Jane. That was the plus and minus of it. He took Jane outta the Bronx and to this fine old house in St. Louis, but he'd filled her svelte body with more chirren than a she-heifer in heat should ever know. He kept her in nice clothes, took her to Paris and Savannah, no, Havana, that was it. Havana. And he was a hard-working soul, the Lord could attest to that. Why, he worked day and night just to keep all those chirren looking right, and Jane in those hats she loved so much, with veils and feathers and sequins.

Vida turned to go indoors, but the breeze tickled her ankles a wee bit, reminding her: once she was courted and treated real sweet. Once she was courted and swept off her feet in a dingy ol' roadhouse out on the islands where her folks woulda died had they known she was parading in hose and satin where throats got cut and women were easily had. Yes, Greer would bring her something nice and she could fan herself on the front porch recollecting the magnolia and the spanish moss where Frank would hide her in the night for one small kiss. In those times a kiss was very personal. Very committin, like a ring, or a first waltz.

Vida lilted through the house to the front porch like she was waltzing in Frank's very arms, and saw Betsey running down the street to the school. Was good the school was right cross the street, that way Vida could keep her eyes on every one of her younguns.

The Judge was backing out his driveway, the chauffeur was opening the door for the museum man to go see over all them crypts from Egypt and the busts from Greece, the rich lady was taking her rich white little girl to the rich little school for the likes of tow-headed smart-alecks. Betsey'd picked up more than a few bad ways from that gal. Betsey didn't know yet that white folks could get away with things a Negro'd be killed for. That's what was wrong with this integration talk, it made the children believe in things that just weren't possible. It was best to be the best in the colored world, and leave the white folks to their wanton ways.

Vida hummed to herself, "Lord, I wanna be a Christian in my soul," and sat rocking on the pillared front porch. Miss Pittypat couldn't of done better. Jane had never had to say "I'll never be hungry again," cause Vida'd seen to it that every one of her chirren ate. Every single one of em. All seven. Huhuh-uhmm, maybe wasn't Jane's fault she was so fulla blossom chirren, maybe she took after her mother. Still, that first picture she saw of Greer was most like a monkey-man she'd ever seen. Greer, jet black in his little monkey hat, talking bout bebop or bopbe, some music that a man he callt Bird jingled outta a saxophone. A monkey man in a monkey hat done run off with her daughter and that was that. Four chirren and God only knew how many more. Please, Lord, no more. Thy Bounty Is Mightily Received. Vida swayed in the wicker chair like the lily of a woman she was, amber-ivory skinned, elegance in the morning.

The street grew still, cept for the slurring oaks and jays in the winds. Everybody who had somewhere to go had gone. Brick houses, ranging from sun-yellow to night maroon, etched the walks and the maids swept the stairs as if dirt were a sin. Soon the housewives would saunter back and forth cross fences, sharing gossip and recipes or the plain old doldrums of living in the roses as they did. Haitians, East Indians, Ricans, and prize-fighters' wives went on bout their business: being beautiful and fertile. Weren't many places the likes of them could live in St. Louis and know the nooks and covies of fifteen- and twenty-room houses. Weren't many places the likes of them could be themselves and raise their children to own the world, which was the plan never spoken.

TWO

St. Louis considered itself the only civilized city on the Mississippi, after New Orleans, of course. Every boulevard bespoke grandeur and Europe, for even the colored avenues weren't without some token frenchified accent. The Civil War accounted for most of the monuments in and about the colored section, and the buildings were graced in marble and granite, as if the nappy or straightened heads and many-hued skins simply had no implications. Betsey's school was sucha place. A great red brick edifice covering more than a block, taking in the colored children from behind the library, cross the trolley tracks, behind the rich girls' school, and back across to the colored teachers' college. All these rushing, giggling brown babies loaded with books and language all their own converged upon Clark Street each morning: one mass of curls and prepubescent excitement.

Betsey was hurrying up the stairs where Twanda was directing up & down traffic, putting the third-graders in their places and looking like Ma Rainey in a fluorescent yellow tent. Twanda's mama did hair the old-fashioned way and wouldn't allow her to comb out the bumper curls till the end of the week. But Twanda was so big, a real big gal, nobody said a word bout how howling funny she be looking. A big black roll of a girl covered up in them big roller curls. Liliana and Mavis twitched in they tight skirts with them slits up the back a little higher than was the usual style: so fast in the seventh grade.

"Charlie gon' give she some, come t'morrow. Betcha money on it. He gointa the high school. Now, how he be in the high school an' he aint gon' give she some?"

But what's he gonna give her? Liliana and Mavis were right in front of Betsey, talking the talk she couldn't make sense of. All Betsey knew was that she was going to give this poem for her very life and win that prize. Huhmph, what was the prize? Betsey wisht it was a trip to Paris, but she knew better. Maybe the prize was a brand-new book, Countee Cullen, or a Paul Robeson record. Wow! Stop thinkin' on the prize. Think on the poem.

"I'ma tell ya one mo' time. If she aint give it up yet, she a fool. Who you think don't want Eugene Boyd?"

Betsey dropped her books at the mention of Eugene Boyd's name. Liliana turned round like someone who had been purposefully provoked:

"Girl, what'sa matter with you? Get holdt to them books and act grown. Don't you let them books get no run in my stockings, ya hear me?"

Betsey was shivering, she was blushing, she was all thumbs; the books wouldn't get back in her arms. "Speak up Ike, an' 'spress yo'self" and Eugene Boyd danced up and down the stairs, but it was Twanda waving her huge arms over Betsey's head, screaming at her.

"Get a move on, rhiney heifer! Whatchu think this is, you' desk? I got traffic to move heah!"

Betsey thought she was gonna cry or faint. She wanted Liliana and Mavis to like her, but here she'd made them mad. Now Twanda was shouting so the whole school could hear. "Rhiney heifer," that's all she needed, a new nickname. How could a rhiney heifer invite Ike or anybody else to speak on anything, much less to come on round, please?

Liliana and Mavis were long gone by the time Betsey gathered her thoughts, her books, her crush on the basketball player, Eugene Boyd. He was like another poem to her. She didn't know him but she "read" him the way you read poems. She watched his every move; the way his blue-gray eyes took in the ankles of all the girls. She knew he liked ankles. She tried to imagine inviting Eugene Boyd to come on in, but she got so excited she whispered out loud: "I'd better stick with Ike."

Not only were the floors of the Clark School shining like the halls of Tara, but Betsey's brow was weeping with sweat, as were her panties and underarms. She imagined she shone like an out-of-place star in midday. She felt hot. And there was Mr. Wichiten with the razor strap at the head of the hallway, justa swinging and smiling.

"Good morning, Elizabeth," Mr. Wichiten murmured, justa swinging and smiling. Betsey knew she'd get a licking with that ol' razor strap with the holes in it if Mr. Wichiten had any idea what was on her mind. Eugene Boyd and Ike, the prize, what "she" gon' give up, who was "she" anyway? Oh, Mrs. Mitchell was not goin to be in a good mood today. She'd never win the prize. There'd be no trip to Paris, no Paul Robeson, and Eugene Boyd would never lay no serious eyes on nobody called "rhiney heifer."

Soon as she'd passt Mr. Wichiten—Praise Be to the Lord—dumb Butchy Jones came rubbing himself up behind her. Betsey dropped her books again, but this time she screamed: "You nasty lil niggah, keep yo' hands off me." And here came Mr. Wichiten, strap justa swinging, Mr. Wichiten justa smiling.

"What's the problem, Elizabeth? You never use language like that."

By this time Butchy was nowhere to be seen and Betsey's books were strewn all over the floor as if she'd lost something on the order of her mind.

"Mr. Wichiten, Sir." It was very important to say "Sir" to the likes of Mr. Wichiten, who had not quite gotten used to the fact that his marvelous principalship was over a horde of colored, and only so many white children as you could count on your fingers.

"Mr. Wichiten, Sir, Butchy did, uh . . . I can't explain what he did exactly, Sir, but it wasn't nice and I got scared. I said bad words to make him go away cause that's all he could understand, Sir."

Mr. Wichiten looked about slowly for the shadow of a creature Elizabeth Brown was calling Butchy and saw nothin. He knew she was probably telling the truth, but with Negro children, no matter what ilk, there's always that shady side.

That strap justa swinging in his hand, Mr. Wichiten stared at Betsey till tears liked ta fall. "I don't care what happens to you in these halls, you come to me before you let the words I heard come from your mouth. Is that understood?"

Betsey nodded yes, picking up her books. Now, she was going to be late for Mrs. Mitchell. Whoever heard of telling a white man anything first? Jesus! Betsey ran, which was also against the rules, to her class. She had to get to "Ike."

Mrs. Mitchell was not happy even before Betsey entered the room in her sweat and anger at Butchy and Mr. Wichiten. Plus, Liliana didn't say who Eugene was messin with. There were so many things going on. Liliana sat with her legs wide open so Willie Ashington could look up her panties. Mavis was writing love notes to Seymour, who was staring at her breasts which weren't quite breasts, but pecans. Mrs. Mitchell's hands were already full when Betsey came in, dripping wet and late.

"Well, I see you've decided to come to class after all."

"Yes, M'am."

"Is it raining outside?"

"No, M'am."

The whole class tittered, watching Betsey answer up to Mrs. Mitchell, who was a smallish woman with a hump in her back. Must have come from carrying too many books. Anyway, Mrs. Mitchell was mighty little and had taught at the Clark School since Adam, or that how folks put it.

But Mrs. Mitchell had watched the children come and go from her classes, 7A and 7B, with delight and dismay. There were years she'd had genius and years she'd been burdened with slow learners, or no learners at all, like Liliana and Mavis and that terrible Butchy, as he called himself. She hadn't reacted like some of the rest when the school turned over from white to black. No, Mrs. Mitchell liked children; she liked young minds. Today, she'd have her regular Elocution Contest, just as she'd had in the past when the girls warbled Byron or Shakespeare and the boys Twain and Stevenson. Today she'd hear something different. Today her students were different. Some of them had been in St. Louis only a day, others a year, few more than a generation. She changed as they changed, and Dunbar, Hughes, and Fawcett were the champions of her new charges. Still, there was this matter of Elizabeth Brown, all wet and late.

"Go to the corner, dear, and calm yourself. I have some talcum in my drawer you may use."

Betsey slid to the back of the room where the encyclopedias were lined up and the complete works of all the white people right underneath. Norman Little whispered to Charlotte Ann that Mrs. Mitchell needed to put some of that talcum on her twat. Mrs. Mitchell heard that and slapped his knuckles good with a long, long ruler she never let go of. She pointed with it, spanked with it, cuddled, cudgeled and directed with it.

To Mrs. Mitchell's surprise her Negro students dug up Whittier and Dickinson, Robinson and Kipling, just as her taffetaed debutantes had thirty years before. Only those two ruffians, Liliana and Mavis, in unison had disrupted the elegance of the program talking about:

He was the boss
Cause he had the sauce
When he put it in
A lil baby dropped in

Mrs. Mitchell was not at all impressed, but Betsey felt something else rising up in her. Listening to Mavis and Liliana, she knew how to speak to Ike, how to get him to express hisself, even if she did have to wear socks instead of stockings. Least she was in the grade she was 'sposed to be, not like Liliana and Mavis, who'd moved far in other directions and were put back each semester. Liliana wore hints of forbidden make-up, while Mavis kept her slip peeking thru her blouse. In those days a silk or, more likely, a rayon scarf was a sign of grown-up-ness, if tied round the neck like a cowboy, though not suggesting anything cowboyish.

Her companion of thirty-six inches nestled under her arm, Mrs. Mitchell asked, "Are you ready with your presentation, Miss Brown?"

"Yes, M'am."

Betsey took her turn, having learned while watching Liliana and Mavis, who were swiftly slapped on their behinds with Mrs. Mitchell's ruler, that "it" had something to do with Ike and Eugene Boyd. Betsey couldn't see anything but Eugene Boyd's eyes and those legs of his that flew in the air when the ball went through the basket. "Who dat knockin at de do'?" took on a more coquettish tease than Betsey'd ever revealed. Yes, there was sucha thing as a mighty love, but who would want a seventh-grader with rhiney skin and only five hairs on that special place where you get "it"? Whatever "it" was? "It" must be very good, the way Liliana talked.

With her "Hmph!" Mrs. Mitchell gave Betsey the first prize, a bunch of red roses from her garden. The first place for a boy went to the one white boy in the class, Richard Singleton, whose burly rendition of "O Captain, My Captain" musta moved Mrs. Mitchell's heart, cause Skeeter Woods and Earl McFee had done real fine on "If We Must Die" by Claude McKay. That probably didn't move Mrs. Mitchell's heart the right way, though. Betsey let her flowers sit on the piano during singing and math. At recess she pulled one out and pushed it into her hair. Maybe Eugene Boyd would see her and ask her where she got such a beautiful rose. What boy from round this way would think to give her one?

After school Charlotte Ann, Veejay, and Betsey ran round to Mr. Robinson's for an ice cream soda and to watch the boys from Soldan High School catch the trolley. Now these weren't the stars of track, basketball, or football, but they were still boys. It could take forever to finish one of Mr. Robinson's sodas, especially if one of the boys from Soldan came into the pharmacy for a leg brace or a notebook, or justa piece of candy. Sometimes Charlie would pass by and scream through the window where the chocolates were displayed, "Betsey is boy crazy." Everybody would look around trying to see who she was, but Betsey would have hidden down under the counter by then. But today with her roses, Betsey sat regally, most arrogant, with the chocolate in her straw tickling her tongue. She smiled when Charlie tried to embarrass her. Thank God he didn't know about Eugene Boyd.

Up from Mr. Robinson's is where Susan Linda lived. She was po' white trash according to Vida, but Charlotte Ann with her braids wound round her head, Veejay with her hair long as a minute and red, and Betsey with this strange rose sticking through an almost ponytail sauntered on over to Susan Linda's to play double-dutch and watch Susan Linda's brothers work on their motorcycles. Tom and Billy Bob had tattoos all up and down their arms and grease under their nails, which was a sure sign of poor upbringing, but Susan Linda's mother was never home and the girls could talk about things and look at each other without fear of being callt names or punished for being brazen. The issue this day was Susan Linda's concerns about hair coming from underneath her arms that was a different color from the tawny blonde hair on her head and distinctly different from the auburn hair inching round her "honey pot" as she liked to call it. Tom and Billy Bob told her that was her honey pot. Betsey wondered if hers was a honey pot, or if that only applied to white girls.

Susan Linda lived on Cabanne Street, which was round the corner from Betsey's and down from the Catholic girls' school. The houses lay back from the curb squished together, like so many windows and porches shouldn't exist where folks passing by could see them. Tom and Billy Bob kept their machines all over the place, and beer cans dotted the side porch insteada begonias or carnations like where Betsey lived. Susan Linda's mother worked in a restaurant, that's why she wore white. Betsey knew that colored women wore white only if they were maids, hairdressers, or nonsurgical nurses. Susan Linda's mother didn't like the colored, so the three girls had to be gone before she got home from flipping flapjacks and hash browns at the twenty-four-hour breakfast place she worked, "For Whites Only."

But there was a serious problem Susan Linda had this day and she hustled Charlotte Ann, Veejay, and Betsey upstairs to her flat to examine it. One of her raspberry nipples was bigger than the other. Susan Linda pullt up her blouse and sure enough it was true. The left nipple was definitely bigger than the right. Betsey felt sorry for her. Charlotte Ann suggested rubbing roses and garlic on the littler one. Veejay blushed through her India-black cheeks. What was the point of looking on yourself so. It was a sin. She knew it was a sin. Susan Linda invited everyone to touch both nipples to see if they felt different, as well as looking strange. Betsey and Charlotte said they felt the same, but Veejay would have none of it.

"Y'all calling on the wrath of God, feelin on each other like that. You better quit or somethin terrible gon' happen. I know. I swear fo' God, I know."

Veejay fled as if the Devil were on her tail when the girls started counting their pubic hairs. Susan Linda, who had most, rolled hers up in tiny pink spoolies with setting lotion, so they'd be pretty. Betsey knew she only had five, but she thought she saw another one trying to sprout up. A lil black dot that was gonna make her more a honey pot. No, she thought, she liked the idea of a lily pot or a rose pot. Some kinda flower that smelled good. Charlotte Ann had ten hairs, but they were so spread apart and soft that Susan Linda couldn't roll them. So she brushed them and oiled them real good with her mama's cold cream. When they finished their anatomical explorations and beautification, Susan Linda put a dab of perfume on everybody and asked them to leave quickly cause her mother'd be walkin in the door any moment and weren't no "niggahs" 'sposed to be in the house.

Betsey knew there was something wrong with that. She and Charlotte Ann always let Susan Linda come over to their houses. Veejay scoffed at them. "Y'all so dumb. Don't you know bout prejudice? It's when white folks don't like Negroes. Didn't you hear that gal call us niggahs. Now, that there is a bad word. My mama tol' me don' 'ssociate wit nobody callin me no niggah, not even colored what does it."

Deep inside, Betsey knew that Veejay was right. They should "boycott" Susan Linda for a while. That's what they were doing in Montgomery, boycotting the white folks till they came round. Papa read the news to her every night bout the Negroes and the whites and the boycotts and standing up for the race, but Susan Linda was so much fun and they were friends. It was too complicated. Betsey shook her head as if she were shaking off her color and all these problems not being white made. Why, there was the sky and clouds that bubbled up in huge towers above her head, and soil smelling of tomatoes or sage, the warmth of the sun on her arms, and here she had to worry bout white folks too? No, not today. Betsey waved bye to her compatriots and made off for her favorite secret place that no one knew was a secret place cause you could see it, if you looked, real easy.

Nestled in her private cranny made by two wide boughs of the ancient tree at the corner of the house, Betsey laid her roses in a circle round her head, a halo of flowers befitting a princess, she thought. The huge oak sprawled over her front lawn, letting the shadows make lacework on the grass and the porch below. The uppermost branches stretched past her very own window, so Betsey knew this was her tree, where she could think all kinds of thoughts and feel all kinds of feelings. She thought on Little Rock and the true crackers down there in the South. Though Grandma said there was crackers every which way you turned. Mama said it was about time. Papa said it wasn't time enough. Papa got real mad and stormed out the room every time the soldiers took those children to the school. He would be saying something on the order of, "Someday they'll see what's right. Someday they'll get what's coming to them."

The first time Betsey saw the soldiers and the mothers like Susan Linda's mother screaming at nine little black children, she threw up all over the floor. Vida got in a tither bout how the colored should leave well enough alone. There wasn't no point in bothering with trash no how. Besides, look at what it'd done to Betsey, upsetting her so, she couldn't hold food down. Betsey thought on those thoughts and bout what she'd do if a crowd of crackers came cursing her and throwing eggs on her pressed clothes. She thought and tears came to her eyes. She'd be 'fraid is what, but Papa said a struggle makes you not afraid, yet Betsey's tree and she weren't assured of that.

With the early evening breeze Grandma came out on the porch to rock and tend her flowers. Grown-ups started driving back up into their driveways and the children came from every direction to greet their parents who'd been off all day working somewhere they let colored work. Next door they was speaking French and down two houses they were Hindi, which was really romantic to Betsey. The nice thing bout segregation was the colored could be all together, where the air and the blossoms were their own, as clear as it was impossible for white folks to put a veil over the sun.

Betsey always felt better when Papa came home. Then he'd play Machito or Lee Morgan. Sometimes he'd put on the colored radio and listen to the blues or turn Bo Diddley way up high. Betsey loved Jackie Wilson. She couldn't wait to see Jackie Wilson in person. She'd heard he took half his clothes off and threw them to the girls who loved him the most. After Jackie Wilson, Betsey wanted to see Ben E. King, so she could let him sing "Stand by Me" just to her. Then she wanted to see Smokey Robinson, but he was in Detroit.

Betsey sat in her tree just thinking away when Jane and

Greer pulled up. Home at last. But Greer just waved to the children who'd come running and left Jane by the front stairs with a mess of groceries. Greer honked the horn as he drove off. Betsey could hear Little Willie John blaring from the car radio. That must have been the reason Jane was shaking her head so. Jane could only take so much common Negro music. Just so much of it, and then she'd had enough.

As she looked down the driveway, Jane put her hands on her hips underneath her suit jacket, closed her eyes, looked bout to cry. When Betsey'd looked around to the back of the house, she saw why her mother was in sucha state. Two big white police were walking Allard and Charlie up the back driveway. Trouble. Trouble. Vida could feel it and came hustling to the back, peering through the screen door.

Jane believed she could feel her blood flowing. Police in the South meant lynchings and beatings and the deaths of Negroes, while white folks laughed. Fire-bombings and burning crosses. Police in the South meant danger to her. Now, her two boys, well, Charlie might as well be her boy, were being escorted up the driveway by two huge red-faced white policemen. In New York she would have called them cops, but here in St. Louis, she knew they were police, just like she knew to say "Sir."

Charlie and Allard, who'd been riding with him on his new three-speed bike, didn't look Jane in the eye, and with good cause. Charlie'd decided to reel and free-hand himself and his little cousin all over the grounds of the Catholic girls' school. Up and down the hills, round the Virgins, flesh and statue, through the rows of nuns on the way to chapel and up and down the stairs of the dormitories. Oh, Charlie'd had a grand time, and the priests had called the police cause not only was it trespassing, but colored weren't allowed to do anything at that place, not even the cleaning. Irish ladies with rose-colored hair and graying faces did that. They were pleasant enough, but only if you minded to stay in your place.

"Good afternoon, M'am. These boys here your younguns?" The biggest police, with black curly hair that most covered the pockmarks on his face, spoke.

"Why, yes, Officer. They are."

"Well, they been riding on private property at the Catholic school round the way, M'am. That's trespassing."

"I see," Jane answered, her face as red as the white folks'.

"I can tell by the looks of you and hereabouts, that you all's not from here, but I wanta letya know we don't take to nigras goin out their way to be in our way, if you know what I mean, M'am."

"No, we aren't from around here."

"Well, on accounta you special, in a sense, we are gointa let these boys by this time, but only this once."

"Thank you, Sir." Jane wanted to pull the posts from the porch and beat the policemen to death. Talkin bout nigras and ways down here and special. As they went on their way, she grabbed Charlie and Allard to her, thanking God they hadn't whistled at some girl like poor Emmet Till.

"Charlie, you a delinquent. You a fool up round them white girls. Must be you like white tail," Margot shouted off the second-story porch, where her mother's hands couldn't reach her. Vida was mumbling round the collard greens and fatback that there had never been no trouble with the law in her family. Never nothing to do with the law. As they passed under her tree, Betsey heard the police talking under their breath bout how different all the children looked, how was more than darkies in somebody's bed. But they were special kinda nigras, not them common types of colored.

"Charlie and Allard gonna go to jail," Sharon taunted.

"All of you be quiet! Do you hear me? Be quiet."

"Well, how do you expect them to act, when you at work all day and they never see their father. You all put too much store by making money. One of you should be back here looking after these chirren."

"Mama, not now. Please, not now."

"Well, when you going to do something about these chirren? When they all in jail?"

"Charlie's a hoodlum," Margot screamed down the back steps.

"Shut up, Margot. Allard, zip your fly. Charlie, go wash your face. Everything's going to be awright." Turning to Charlie, Jane said, "We'll talk when Uncle Greer gets home."

"When Greer gets home, all these chirren woulda been in the bed."

"Mama, please, not now."

"Well, it's your house."

"Yes, it is."

With that Vida rubbed her eyes which were tearing and pulled her apron to her chest as she walked to her room. No one took her seriously. No one understood what the children needed, especially colored chirren, when them white folks be in they crazy ways.

Jane sat at the kitchen table, gazing blankly at the cupboard where she kept the regular china and the keepsakes from Great Aunt Jane: two candelabra and a crystal butter dish. Jane couldn't get it through her head why Greer was never home when everything went crazy. As she recalled, fathers were supposed to take care of police and discipline and order. "I swear I can't do this by myself. Good lord, I can't do this by myself." Jane lit a candle for Aunt Jane's memory and was about to pray on her situation when Betsey touched her shoulder.

"Mama, what kinda nigra is a special kinda nigra, and aren't they supposed to call us Negroes?"

"Yes, Betsey. And no, I don't know what kinda nigra is a special kinda nigra. But you're right, darling, we are Negroes with a capital N."

Jane hugged her daughter, hoping Betsey didn't know all she could do about the Negro problem was set the table for dinner.

THREE

"God dammit, Greer! Do you understand anything I ever say to you?"

Jane looked at her wedding picture, satiny, a patina of thirteen years veiling her young foolish face. She wanted to push the gilded edges of the damn thing through Greer's head the way he used scalpels to take bullets outta the hoodlums he loved so much.

"Did you hear me? Where were you when I needed you? Me? Jane, your wife! Not some lowly sick acting-the-fool stinking niggahs so dumb they can't find the goddam clinic! Do you hear me? I am talking to you!"

Greer looked up from *Digest for Surgical Procedures* and nodded his head. Jane froze. She held her breath and started again. She was going to be decent about this one more time.

"Where were you when the police brought our children home? Don't you realize what could have happened to them? Where were you, dammit! Answer me!"

Jane picked up his stethoscope and threw it at him. Greer caught it in his left hand and went right on reading.

"I was at the Johnsons'. He's been bleeding again since he left the hospital and I wanted to check on him. He's an old man, Jane, he can't get up and run to the clinic on one leg."

"But I suppose your children could be in jail or dead on accounta poor Mr. Johnson, who's got so many benefits he's forgotten what money looks like."

Jane walked round the bed to Greer and pulled the *Digest* from his hands. "Did Mr. Johnson pay you something today? Or you so holy you can give your services away? Who do you think you are, St. Francis? I have a house full of children who need clothes, shoes, dental work, eyeglasses, dance classes, food, and a father. And where is their father? Why, seeing Mr. Johnson! Mr. Johnson doesn't live here, Greer. We live here with five children and my beloved mother who was right that the race definitely needs some improving!"

Jane began to beat the dresser with the *Digest*. Then she started tearing it to pieces, when Greer slowly wrapped her in his arms, saying: "Aren't the boys all right?" Jane didn't respond. "Aren't the police going to leave them alone, if they act right?" Jane said nothing. "Look, honey, they're not in jail. Charlie was just having a little fun."

"Charlie was having fun, was he? Well, this is St. Louis, Missouri, my dear. You ask Chuck Berry how much fun the police let Negroes have when it comes to white girls." Jane snatched Greer's loosened tie from round his neck.

"I am going to tell you one more time. I cannot run this house as if I were the father and the mother. Now I know you are a doctor, and you have a public responsibility, but if you don't put this household first in your life, I swear 'fore Jesus you're going to be in for a big surprise."

Greer knew Jane in these moods. He didn't understand why she couldn't see he was working himself half to death to keep the family exactly the way she wanted. She didn't understand that poor colored people didn't get decent treatment at the clinic, and by going by to see them he was building a clientele for his real practice. Damn, Greer thought, for such an intelligent woman, Jane didn't have much foresight.

"I got home as soon as I could." With that, Greer took his tie out of Jane's hands and picked up the latest issue of *MD Magazine*.

Jane sat at her vanity table staring at Greer, who had the audacity to read when her boys had been touched by southern police. What gall! What an ass she'd married! What ever was she going to do? She took the emery boards from the top left drawer and started doing her nails. She was going to play bridge, but before she did that she was going to have a scotch and soda and play a game of solitaire with the prettiest hands a woman with this many problems could have. Not another word passed between them, not one that was spoken, at any rate, not a word anyone else would understand.

Betsey thought she understood it. She thought she knew that the problem was there were too many of them. Too many children. Too wild. Too much noise. Too trying for her delicate mother's nature. Why, Mama wasn't raised to tend to a bunch of ruffians like Sharon and them, especially not Charlie, who'd awready been put out of schools in the north. No, Betsey knew when her parents were arguing it was most likely on accounta the children. Then there was the problem of the white people and money. White folks and money seemed to go hand in hand. Whenever a Negro mentioned one, he mentioned the other, like the white folks had took up all the money and were hiding it from the Negroes, like they kept the nice houses for themselves, and the good schools, and the restaurants and motels. Just for themselves.

"You did not win," Charlie screeched down the back stairs. The basketball ricocheted from one wall to the other all the way down the stairway.

"Betsey! Would you see what's the matter," Jane called tiredly from her manicure and highball.

"He did too!"

"He didn't." Margot and Sharon began tustling with each other over the issue of whether or not Allard had won, when it was clear it was none of their business.

"He didn't what?" Betsey screamed into the house from her terrace, where she'd gone to escape the chaos of the house.

"Betsey! Didn't I ask you to see about these children?" Jane leapt up, exasperated. "Betsey, where are you?"

"That's not yours." Margot tried to pull the ball and jacks from Sharon.

"Who threw this ball down the stairs?" Vida hollered up.

"I don't know, Grandma," Betsey hollered down.

"Well, come along here and get it. It certainly doesn't belong in the kitchen."

"Grandma, I didn't have anything to do with that ball!"

"I'ma tell on you. You pull my hair one more time, ya hear?"

"Give it back then."

"I will not either."

"Allard, put those matches down! I see you. Where'd you start the fire?" Betsey ran after Allard, who'd only set a small fire on the third floor to get back at Charlie who was a big bully anyway. By the time Betsey'd put the fire out, the second floor was going crazy.

"I'ma tell Mama. You tore my dress."

"If you do, I'ma knock one of those buck teeth of yours out!"

"Where's my basketball?"

"I'ma tell Mama."

"Mama, Mama, please make her stop."

"Mama, please make her stop."

"Mama, Allard got holdt to some matches again, but everything's awright."

"Sharon, stop it. I say."

"You're hurtin my arm!"

"Mama, please, come help me," Margot cried.

"Mama, she's lying on me," Sharon moaned.

"Mama, I didn't start a big fire," Allard explained.

"Aunt Jane, tell Grandma to give me back my basketball."

"Mama, please! Come help."

Jane shut the door to her room and played solitaire, betting against herself. Greer'd fallen asleep. He'd been on call two nights in a row. Betsey went to her terrace for some cloud peace and air. The children just went on like children will do. Jane's thoughts veered to her wedding vows, "in sickness and in health." Wasn't anything about in madness or white folks.

Betsey took a deep breath cause the South may be full of ugly things but it's not in the air. The air is flowers, leaves and spaces divine, when you're up high enough to climb onto a sturdy branch of your very own oak tree. If she climbed out to the middle of the tree, Betsey thought, she'd be a bird and sing a colored child's bird song, a colored child's blues song or a hot jump and rag song. From the middle of her tree, where she was sure she was not supposed to be, Betsey listened real close for her city to sing to her so she could respond. Everybody knows any colored child could sing, specially one from a river city. A hankering blues-ridden, soft-swaying grace of a place like her home would surely answer her first melody.

From her vantage point through the myriad leaves, Betsey saw what looked to her mind like a woman in need of some new clothes and a suitcase. Who ever heard of carrying one's belongings in two shopping bags, while wearing a hat with five different colored flowers on it? And she was singing a Mississippi muddy song:

humm hum, hum hum, hum uh

well, my name is bernice & i come a long way
up from arkansas & i'm here to stay
i got no friends & i aint got no ma

but i'ma make st. louis give me a fair draw

hum hum, hum hum, hum hum, uh

there's some pretty young men
in these mighty fine jobs
got pomade in their hair
& they move like the light
i'ma set my sights
on a st. louis guy
with some luck by my side
i'ma dress up my best
& bring me a st. louis mess of a man

humm hum, hum hum, hum hum, hum uh

i'ma show them white folks in arkansas
that a good woman can get what she want
how she want and when/ humm humm, humm humm

my name is bernice & i come a long way
i'ma makin my business in st. louis to stay

The song moved as if it weren't usedta having shoes on its feet. The lips blurred like the slurs of her lines, losing definition into flat pimply cheeks and a head of hair in need of pressing underneath that hat. Bernice hadda way about her. A country honor that came from knowing hard work too soon, and being rid of it too late. The children's noises coming from this big ole house gladdened her heart.

"I told you to give me my jacks!"

"No ball playing beneath the chandelier, do you hear me, you piece of northern trash! Even if you are my grandchild, you aint right."

"Mama, Mama, please come see to Sharon."

"Jane, you best come out your room and see to these chirren 'fore they tear your house down."

Bernice waddled up the stairs from the curb, glanced at Betsey in the tree, took a breath and hummed her song. She had been walking round this rich colored neighborhood all day looking for work, and she was determined to stay in St. Louis. She was going to help this family out. She was what was missing, an eye on these hincty misbehaving brats. Bernice kept on up the stairs to the front door in time to the yelps and hollers careening through the screens of every floor. Seemed like not a child in there could talk decent. All of them screaming and hollering like they were out on the farm. Bernice rang the front door bell.

"Mama, there's somebody at the door."

"Mama, there's a colored woman at the door."

"Mama, there's a fat lady at the door."

"Jane, you've got a visitor."

"Aunt Jane, there's something at the door."

Jane tied her robe round her waist, while looking at Greer asleep in his clothes. That damned green surgical outfit sprawled all over her fresh linen. But that was the man she'd married. She bent over and gave him a peck of a kiss, a long caress where the evening shadow was beginning to appear on his chin.

"Jane, I say, you've got a caller!"

By the time Jane reached the front door, all the children were crowded round her like the woman who lived in a shoe. It was claustrophobic. She had a hard time opening the front door for all the feet pressed up against it. What she saw was a heavyset, no-funny-business country woman with the most peculiar hat.

"Good evening, M'am."

"Yes, may I help you? I'm Mrs. Brown."

"Yes, M'am, Mrs. Brown. I see you've got some chirrens and I thought you might be in need of some he'p. I'ma hardworkin gal. I come up from Arkansas to raise myse'f up. I'm ready to tend after em, and see to they meals and hair and such."

Jane smiled, thinking the Lord moves in mysterious ways.

"Well, come in, Miss, uh . . ."

"My name is Bernice Calhoun, M'am."

"Well, Miss Calhoun, please come in. This is Allard. Here is Sharon. This is Margot. And my nephew Charles. Oh, I wonder where Betsey is? Mama, have you seen Betsey?" Jane called.

"No, I haven't," Vida answered from the kitchen.

"Miss Calhoun, have you worked with children before?"

"Why, yes, M'am, in Arkansas."

"Do you have any references you could show me?"

"Well, I could tell you the names of the families I worked for, and you could call them. But down south they's mighty informal, so I don't have anything writ down that I could show you."

"Oh my." Jane sighed. "I think the best thing to do, Miss Calhoun, is for you to give me the names and addresses of your former employers. I shall write them. In the meantime, you may work here on a probationary basis, till I've heard from them."

"Oh, that's fine, M'am."

Vida was approaching Jane to say she had no idea where Betsey was. Instead she interrupted, "Who's this?"

"Oh, Mama, this is Bernice Calhoun, who's going to stay on to help with the children. Isn't that wonderful? Miss Calhoun, this is my mother, Mrs. Murray."

Vida took one look at Bernice and went back to the kitchen, shaking her head about what the race had to offer.

"I can't figure out where Betsey is right now, Bernice, but she's my oldest girl and she'll be a big help to you."

Bernice pursed her lips, thinking now would be the time to get in good with Mrs. Brown. Show her what a sharp eye she had for chirrens.

"Might she be that one out there, up in that tree, M'am?"

Jane forgot the time of day. She stiffened and ran out on the front porch to the far end. Right above her head, in the middle of a huge tree, sat her daughter, Betsey.

"Betsey, you come down from there right this instant! How do you expect to set an example behaving like a jackass? Come down from there, right this minute! Do you hear me, Elizabeth!"

When Jane called Betsey "Elizabeth," it was serious. Betsey cut her eyes at Bernice Calhoun, who didn't realize what a mistake she'd made. Honeying up to Jane wasn't going to do her any good. Jane wasn't home half the day, Betsey Brown was. Now, Betsey Brown was more than mad cause some fool Mississippi song had given away her sacred hiding place. Made her mama call her Elizabeth.

"I'll be right out, Mother. I'm so sorry. I can't imagine what got into me." Betsey oozed, not fooling Jane at all. "I want to meet the company. I'm coming right now."

Jane watched in amazement as her daughter maneuvered herself along the limbs of the tree to the edge of the terrace and through the window. In a flash Betsey presented herself.

"Hello, my name is Elizabeth Brown. How are you?"

Jane was proud of her daughter again. Bernice thought she'd made a friend.

"Betsey, I told you, Miss Calhoun."

"Oh, M'am, the chirrens can call me Bernice."

"I told Bernice that you would help her with the children and the running of the house. Show her to her room on the third floor and tell her about the neighborhood and the children's chores."

Betsey took Bernice by the hand. Charlie reluctantly picked up her paper bags filled with God only knew what and up they traipsed through the back stairway to the top of the house. It was against Jane's principles to put a Negro in the basement. It was against the children's principles to accept somebody who was going to tell on them all the time. Betsey had some very special plans for Miss Calhoun.

"I hope you'll be very happy with us, Bernice. The girls are very smart and Allard never causes any trouble and Charlie is practically a grown-up awready."

"Why, thank-ya, 'Liz'beth."

"Uh, Betsey is just fine, Bernice, if you don't mind."

"Well, I say to ya again, thank-ya, Miss Betsey."

Betsey gave the secret sign of a fist behind her back

with two fingers outstretched to indicate it was time for a children's meeting in the basement. Who did this Bernice think she was, giving away secrets like that? Why, Jane didn't even know about the tree reaching over the porch until Bernice came. Betsey was going to see to it that Bernice paid. Boy, would she pay. The line, led by Charlie dribbling the basketball down the stairs, headed straight for the bowels of the house.

Bernice didn't know it, as she examined the tilted curved ceilings of her new quarters. Jane didn't know it, as she curled up next to Greer behind the locked door of their room above the lilacs. Only the children in the darkest smallest corner of the basement knew what Bernice had coming her way. Vida in the kitchen over chicken fricassee could only think of her Frank and how much he liked the meat to fall off the bone over the rice and onions. And there was nothing any one of the grown-ups could have done had they known what was up in the basement.

The basement was a secret of its own. There were rooms that led to other rooms and back round to the first room. There were closets that went way back against the walls of the house until it smelled like the earth was coming right on in. There were rooms to have seances and see cats have kittens. Corners to whisper make-believe apologies and dreams. There was the smell of many folks having lived in the dark for many years, and there was the children's favorite meeting place that no one bigger than them had ever seen. In the far left-hand corner of the longest closet with the lowest ceilings and plywood walls painted green long before Christ was born, the Brown children had their pow-wow.

"How's she gonna do something with us?" Betsey was riled, and her little temper was cavorting in the shadows with her small horde of followers. "She can't even talk. Imagine callin me 'Lizabeth. Why, that aint even a name, 'Lizabeth!"

"And she tol' on you too, Betsey," Sharon chimed in.

"Mama didn't know nothing bout that tree," Margot added.

"Not now, Allard. Now we've got to figure out a way to get this woman out of our house."

"Not only can't she talk, she can't hardly walk," Charlie quipped with the basketball twirling on his finger, then behind his back.

"So how's she gonna do something with us?" Allard decried.

"She's not. Just wait till morning." And Betsey dismissed the crowd.

Betsey was not a vindictive child. She was a child of special places and times of her own. She tried not to hurt anybody or anything, but Bernice'd given the whole family access to her privacy. Now when they went looking for her, they'd all know to go to her beloved tree. Search its branches for the dreamer and make noises that would disrupt Betsey's current reveries. No, Betsey wasn't being evil, to her mind she was protecting herself. God only knew what else that Bernice would uncover and deliver over to Jane and Greer. Heaven forbid she ever found that long closet in the basement! That's where everybody practiced writing nasty words like "pussy" and "dick," though only Charlie admitted to knowing where all these things were. Margot just liked to write them in big red letters with nail polish she'd borrowed from her mother's collection of toiletries. Allard just liked making the letters, and then asking what the word was.

Meanwhile, in the upper reaches of the house, Bernice was hanging her limited wardrobe in the armoire next to a single bed just bout big enough to accommodate her rotund brown body. Yes, she thought, looking at the red dress with the lace on one sleeve, St. Louis was gointa be just fine. She'd have every Friday and Saturday night off, to meet some nice hard-working fella, maybe one of them from down her way, not too citified. Bernice looked out her window down on the garden, thinking how lucky she'd been to run into the Brown family. That poor Mrs. Brown, so frail, with all these chirren, and Mrs. Murray with her nose all up in the air on accounta a body didn't have good hair. She'd win them over. That's what she'd do.

In the morning the children tumbled down the stairs into a fine chaos. First, Betsey told Allard it was alright to rub the goldfish together. Then Sharon and Margot decided to swing on the curtain rod separating the living room from the parlor. Charlie decided he'd practice throwing his basketball around the chandelier. Of course, Jane and Greer were relaxing for a change, relieved to have Bernice handling everything. Even Vida had gone out to see to her dahlias in the back. So it was just Bernice and the Brown children.

"Look Bernice, somebody peed in the bed." Margot came running through the kitchen with a dank sheet wrapped round her head.

"Bernice, you wanta see me make fires? We could use these matches right under here." Allard crawled through Bernice's legs to the cupboard where the fireplace matches were kept. He really liked those. They were so long and the fire was very tiny at first, till you threw it somewhere. Then whamo. Big flame.

Yet Bernice was undaunted. She was gointa stay in St. Louis, no matter what.

"Bring that nappy head on round heah. No, don't carry no comb, bring me a brush. A comb aint gointa go threw all that mess."

Bernice'd made breakfast of grits and eggs that no one ate, claimin the grits were stiff and the eggs too hard.

"Allard, didn't you say you wanted to climb out the window. The one in my room is open. Sharon, there's some money in Bernice's sweater pocket, if you want to buy some Snickers today."

All this was going on while Bernice was trying to make some sense of the mass of braids on the girls' heads. Bernice shouted, "Put them goldfish down. I want my money in my pocket right now." It didn't sit right with her. This Betsey was supposed to be her friend, and here she was undermining everything.

"Bernice, the fish are dying."

"Well, put em back in the water, fool."

"I'ma tell Mama you callt me a fool."

"That's right Allard, you tell Mama."

"Betsey, bring that head over heah, I tol' you."

"Bernice, I'm hungry."

"Well. Eat your breakfast."

"I don't want breakfast, I want some chicken."

"That's for dinner."

"I want some chicken now!"

"Well awright, then. Charlie, get that basketball out this house."

"Oh, Bernice, I spilled all the chicken grease."

Bernice stood up with an Arkansas fire in her eyes screaming, "You better eat them grits cause that's all you gonna get! Put them goldfish down! I tell ya whoever took my money bettah pray for they soul! I aint going nowhere and y'all best mind, cause I'm in St. Louis to stay."

"How you gonna do something with us?"

"You can't even talk."

"I say bring that nappy head on over heah!"

The ruckus sent Jane flying down the stairs to find the blinds at a 45-degree angle in the front room. The curtains in the parlor all over. Six crystals from her chandelier on the floor. Chicken grease on the kitchen floor. A table full of grits and eggs. Not one combed head. Allard with matches in both pockets. Betsey quietly gazing out the window at Vida working with her dahlias. Plus, no one had brought up the morning's coffee. Now this was just too much. No coffee and the house in a shambles. It was better with her mother tending to the children, even though it was hard on her heart. The likes of this never happened.

"And, Miss Calhoun, just what do you call yourself doing this morning?"

"Well, M'am, I fixed the chirren they breakfast. Then I put the chicken on for dinner. Then I was bout to start doing heads, but Betsey told them they could climb through windows and steal my money, take them fish out the water. Oh Mrs. Brown, they been a mess today."

"Bernice, don't you wanta see me make fires?" Allard grinned. Jane grabbed the matches from his hands and all his pockets, slapped his backside good. She turned to Miss Calhoun with Sharon between her legs wrapped up in the wet sheet smelling of urine.

"Miss Calhoun, I just don't think this is going to work out."

At that moment Vida was about to come into the kitchen through the back door. Betsey ran to her aid: "Oh, Grandma, be careful. Bernice left chicken grease all on the floor. You hold onto me or you might slip and fall."

Vida cut her eyes first at Jane, then at Bernice. "Well, I should have known that a body with no upbringing couldn't very well bring up these chirren of mine. Thank you, Betsey, you are always so helpful."

The children ran gleefully to school shouting: "How's she gonna do something with us. She can't even talk. She can't even walk. How's she gonna do something with us."

Bernice sat glumly on her small bed. She felt sucha big fool. Mrs. Brown had let her go in one day, she hadn't even had one Friday night off to wear her red dress. She couldn't hardly begin to pack her things. She heard the folks in Arkansas laughing at her. Big ol' flat-faced Bernice gointa to St. Louis. Hahahaha.

Jane made her own coffee, sat at the kitchen table with the children's breakfasts surrounding her and played a game of solitaire. There was no way in the world she could go to work today. Thank God for Betsey. There was one child with a head on her shoulders. Jane tried to think of what might have happened if Betsey hadn't been there to mind the children.

FOUR

Betsey could hardly wait to tell Veejay and Charlotte Ann what had happened at her house. She wanted to brag that she herself had run old Bernice out the house. When she saw Charlotte Ann talking through the fence to Seymour Bournes, who was from the high school and a friend of Eugene Boyd, she rushed up. Charlotte Ann's eyes were sparkling and her hips were wiggling totally out of control.

"Charlotte Ann, how are you doing? Hi, Seymour," Betsey blurted, full of herself and inquisitive bout the relationship tween Seymour and Charlotte Ann, who'd always said she was ascared of boys, but apparently not this one. Seymour was a tallish boy with curly black hair and large ears that flew from the sides of his head like propellers. They would have looked like ordinary ears had his face been any fuller, but Seymour's face was thin, like a taffy pulled way far out. Seymour had seen Betsey before, but didn't actually know her. Her cousin Charlie played ball real good, but it was Eugene who'd pointed her out to him. Eugene liked her. As a matter of fact, Eugene had taken to being friends with Charlie just so he'd have a reason to visit, but Betsey and Charlotte Ann knew nothing of this. All Charlotte Ann knew was Betsey was beside herself about something that would have to wait till Seymour went cross the street to class.

Betsey saw Veejay coming through the schoolyard with her books up under her left arm, as always chewing gum to make sounds like a popping snare drum. Realizing that Charlotte Ann and Seymour were no longer aware of her, Betsey ran toward Veejay yelling, "Hey, Veejay, guess what?"

"What ya mean, 'guess what'? Can't you say hello or good day or something?" Veejay retorted tween smacks of cherry gum.

"Well, Good Day, then, Miz Veejay, M'am." The two girls laughed and kept on tittering M'ams and Good Mornings till Betsey told Veejay bout Bernice and how bad they'd all been and how Bernice had gotten her walking papers and the house was theirs again. Betsey'd opened her lunch bag awready, chewing on a bright apple, waiting for Veejay to cry out with a "Go on, girl" or "I bet that was a lot of fun," but Veejay was just looking mad and hurt all at once.

"Whatsa matter, Veejay? She's gone now. That's what

counts, isn't it? She told on us. She would have ruined everything."

"Betsey, you know what my mama does for a living?"

"No."

"Well, she takes care of nasty white chirren who act up like y'all acted up this morning. She don't do it cause she likes it neither. She does it so I could have clothes and food and a place to live. That's all that Bernice woman was trying to do, and you so stupid you don't even know if she's got somewhere to live or if she's got chirren of her own in Arkansas. Y'all act like white people, always trying to make things hard on the colored. Lying on em and making a mess of things. Thinking it's so funny. I don't even know if I want to be your friend. That could have been my mama lost her job on accounta you and your ol' tree. You shouldn'ta been up no tree no how, big as you are. You don't have no sense at all."

Veejay turned to go anywhere away from Betsey. She'd known that Betsey was from over there where the rich colored lived, but she liked her anyway. Till now, that is. Now Betsey was the same as anybody who made fun of her mother for doing daywork and looking after white children while her own waited anxiously at the door for her to come home. It was one thing to take mess from white folks, cause that was to be expected, but to have the colored—or the "Negro," as Betsey would say—do it too was hurting to Veejay, who just kept mumbling, "That coulda been my mama and you don't care."

"Veejay, I didn't mean any harm." Betsey rushed alongside Veejay, who wouldn't look at her. "Really, I didn't think, that's all. I'll tell my mother that it was all my fault. I will,

Veejay, I promise. Just please stay my friend." Betsey tugged Veejay's arm, wanting her to stop so they could talk before Mrs. Mitchell quieted the class for morning announcements about Assembly, band practice, girls' volleyball, and the Pledge of Allegiance and the Lord's Prayer.

Veejay stopped. "Take your hands off me. Betsey Brown, you a selfish somebody. I don't want you to call my name. And don't you tell nobody that I'm your friend, or that I ever was, ya hear me."

Veejay stalked off to class, leaving Betsey on the stairwell with a half-eaten apple and a lot on her mind.

It was true that Veejay wore the same plaid skirt and white blouse every other day, but Betsey thought that was cause Veejay wanted it that way. Veejay'd never invited her or Charlotte Ann to visit her at home, either. And it was always Veejay who had words from her mama on what white folks were really like.

A heavy red glow came over Betsey's body. Shame. She was ashamed of herself and her sisters and Charlie and Allard. Veejay was right. Bernice just talked funny was all. Betsey'd passed over the paper bags fulla worn-out clothes, the two shoes of that woven cotton, fraying by the toes, and the calluses on the palms of the woman's hands. Betsey Brown had been so busy seeing to herself and the skies, she'd let a woman who coulda been Veejay's mama look a fool and lose her job.

Betsey threw the apple in the trash and peeked round her carefully. She was gonna run home fast as she could, to see if she could catch her mother and tell her the truth. Maybe there was time to stop Bernice from leaving. Why, Betsey didn't know if Bernice had a girl her own age or not. Betsey didn't know if Bernice had anyplace to go, or anyone to go to. Betsey had to get home and apologize to Bernice.

It was awfully hard to sneak out of Clark School once you were in it. Hall patrols and Mr. Wichiten wandered arbitrarily hither and yon, but Betsey made a good run for it, down the south corridor to the door that opened toward the high school. Sometimes that door was locked or chained to keep out vagrants or bad elements, which really meant gangs, but today the door was open and out Betsey went, praying she'd catch her mother or Bernice to say "I'm sorry, please stay."

But all the running in the world and all the praying in the world couldn't catch up with the misery Bernice Calhoun knew that morning. Bernice was stepping up into the Hodiamont streetcar when Betsey spied her grandma on the front porch chattering with the wind bout what a blessing it was that trashy country gal was gone. How it was goin' to take days to put the house back in order. Betsey backed down from the porch before her grandma could lay eyes on her. Running round the back she saw her mother on her hands and knees cleaning the chicken grease off the floor. Mr. Jeff was in the parlor hanging the curtains back up.

"Betsey, what are you doing home?" Jane asked over her shoulder. Her hands were sudsy and sweat rimmed her brow, but she didn't seem to be in a bad mood like Betsey'd expected.

"I came home to help clean up, Mama, and I wanted to tell you something, too."

"Don't worry, darling, I know you did your best this morning. I'm just going to have to screen these ladies more carefully from now on. Really, Betsey, I don't believe the house has ever been quite this much a mess. All because I didn't check the references, I guess. Can't be too careful nowadays."

"But, Mama, don't you want me to help? It's my fault. I didn't do what you asked me to do."

"Betsey, you go back to school where you belong. I never expected you to run this house all by yourself. That's why I hired that Calhoun woman. But you live and you learn."

"Mama, that's not what I meant."

"Doesn't matter, sweetheart." Jane rose from the floor, wiping her hands on the back of her pants she'd rolled above her knees, and went to the table to write a note. She looked like a teenager, with a scarf over her bangs and a short-sleeved cotton shirt tied at the waist. "Just get along back to school before you're marked truant, okay? Here's a note to give to Mr. Wichiten that says you've been home helping me."

"Mama, it was all my fault."

Jane drew Betsey close to her, tugging her ponytail, and said in a soft voice: "I don't want to hear any more of that, you understand? You did the best you could." With that Jane patted Betsey on the rear: "Off to school with you now. Be good."

Betsey didn't want to go back to school. Veejay'd be there, who usedta be her friend. She didn't want to go to her room either, or the basement where she'd made all the hateful plans to get rid of Bernice. She stole past her mother up the back stairs and out her window to her tree. The same tree that had started it all.

Closer to the sky and clouds, Betsey felt some of the pain wear away. She swore she'd do her best not to hurt or embarrass another Negro as long as she lived. She prayed Bernice would find another place with children not half so bad as she was. She asked God to let Veejay be her friend again. She decided not to go back to school, but to do penance instead. She sat in her tree on her knees till every bone in her body ached. Then she curled up on her favorite branch and wept for having cared so little. It could have been Veejay's mama. Maybe Veejay's mama talked funny too, but that didn't make her less a somebody, or liable to the antics of a whimsical girl who sometimes put dreams before real life, or confused them completely. It was absolutely impossible for her to have anything in common with nasty white children who bothered Veejay's mother. It was absolutely impossible for the colored to have somethin so much akin to the ways of white folks.

Seemed like her tree'd made a cradle for her and rocked her off to sleep. Betsey was nigh on heaven's doorstep with the rustling and caws of the approaching evening, but a foreign motion interrupted her dreams. Swish. Blop. Blop. Swish. Blop. Blop. Charlie and none other than Eugene Boyd were throwing the ball over her curved body through the leaves, the limbs, the wind. Quite a challenge to Charlie's mind: make Betsey the basket and not wake her. That was the game. If his simple-minded cousin sleep in a tree at her age, she deserved whatever a body could think up. Eugene on the other hand had every intention of waking the beauty up. If he needed a basketball, so be it. Charlie took the girl for granted, maybe cause she was his cousin or maybe cause she was not his type. Eugene wasn't exactly dawdling neath the awakening Betsey, who almost lost her balance when she realized that indeed it was the very Eugene Boyd from Soldan leaping up the tree trunk to dunk the ball on the other side of her head.

"What are y'all doing? Do I look like a basketball court to you, Charlie?"

Betsey immediately thought that Charlie'd brought Eugene over just to taunt her and make her look bad. Suddenly she changed her demeanor.

"Hi, Eugene. I'm Bets . . . Elizabeth, Charlie's cousin. He stays with us here. Oh, but I guess you know that awready."

Betsey didn't know what to do. If she climbed down the tree, they'd think she was a tomboy. If she went through her window, she'd lose sight of Eugene. If she stayed where she was, they might knock her out of the tree. Not on purpose, but every shot is not a perfect one, not even for the likes of Eugene Boyd. Betsey sat up where she was, pulling her skirt over her knees to hide the scratch marks and to seem more grown, she thought. At least she wouldn't be up in the tree with her skirt hung up all round her waist like she was ten, or she didn't know that boys liked to look up girls' dresses, big boys too. She knew that cause Charlie talked a lot, but Charlie had disappeared to the back where the real basketball net was justa yearning for him.

"Come on, Gene, let's play ball." Charlie's voice floated round the edge of the house.

Eugene just kept looking at Betsey up on her perch with her hands over her knees and cheeks blushing like strawberries.

"You always stay up there?"

"No, I'm not always up here. I come up here to think is all."

Betsey didn't know what else to say. She didn't want Eugene Boyd to think she was weird. Then, on the other hand, she didn't think it was weird to stay in her tree, comforted and free as she was when boys weren't throwing balls over her head.

"What you thinkin bout up there? Your boyfriend?"

"No, oh, I always think about him when I'm alone. He's so handsome and very tall, but he's not from round here. He's from somewhere else."

"Where? Sumner? Beaumont? I wanna know cause if he's not as good looking as me, or a center forward like me, or nearby, I'd like to be considered, or rather, I'd like to come and visit with you sometime. Unless he's always on your mind."

Betsey perked up. She looked all over the tree for some advice, some indication of what to do next. What should she say? How should she move? Where were her pretty dresses? Wasn't she supposed to have on a glorious dress at a moment like this? Eugene Boyd was at the foot of her tree. This was important.

"Could you wait just one minute? I'll be right down. I'd like to talk to you a little bit longer, if you don't mind. My boyfriend lives far away from here, don't worry about him, okay?"

Betsey somehow finessed her way to the balcony, looking like a trapeze artist. Once she reached it she jumped through her window, onto her bed, about to scream with joy and surprise. Eugene. Eugene Boyd was downstairs. In minutes she'd oiled her legs, twisted her ponytail, washed her face, and put on her Sunday-school dress with the polka dots and the ribbon that tied just beneath her almost breasts. With a giant sigh and a smile right behind it, she took the front stairs very slowly, step by step, as if she were in a wedding procession. Then she forgot herself and skipped every other step, reaching the front door in a very unladylike sweat.

"Hi, here I am."

Betsey waved to Eugene, who was still over by the side of the house looking up at her tree. The two of them were one big smile trying to cover itself up. Charlie'd left Eugene with the ball and gone off on his bike to razz the white girls, but Eugene had found his adventure right on Charlie's front porch.

"What'd you say your boyfriend's name was?"

"Oh, it doesn't matter, believe me. I watched you play the other day. You're so good." Betsey scooped up her skirt and sat on the stoop, while Eugene dribbled and bounced and dunked and turned this way and that, doing his best to impress her and get close to her. He dribbled the ball up and down the steps, asking her questions, like how old she was and did she like to dance and had she ever seen the Shirelles. Betsey was in a sweet daze through most of the conversation. She liked the talk best when Eugene dribbled the ball right next to her dress, so his leg or hand touched her shoulders. She liked the shape of his calf under his pants and the smell of his dampness mixed with the evening's.

"I guess you'll be going when Charlie comes back, huh?" Betsey looked away as she felt out Eugene's intentions.

"Why would I do that, when I came to see you? I see ol' loud-mouthed Charlie every day."

With that Eugene looped the ball round Betsey's back and caught it so his arms were on either side of her, his face directly in front of her. Betsey tried to keep her eyes open. In the movies, people closed their eyes when their faces almost touched, but that was almost kissing and Betsey'd never been kissed. She tried to keep her eyes open and Eugene kept looking in them, coming closer and closer till their lips met and Betsey's eyes closed of their own accord.

This kiss was soft and light, like petals of protea or Thai orchids. This kiss was a river wisp and innocent as dawn. It never stopped. They breathed a little and their lips parted as simply as they'd joined.

Eugene backed up and flung the ball through the air. Betsey lilted about in her glory.

"Maybe I'll come back by here, if it's awright with you? You sure are pretty, too pretty to be Charlie's cousin."

"Oh, if you were to come by, I'm sure I'll be around somewhere."

"What about your boyfriend who's so handsome?"

"Oh, I forgot about that, but don't you worry. He'll never find out. Really, he lives very far away," Betsey cooed, knowing the closest she'd ever come to having a boyfriend was this boy standing right in front of her.

"Betsey—oh, no, I'm sorry—Elizabeth, may I kiss you again? You kiss so good."

Eugene drew up next to Betsey and put his face real close to hers one more time, but Betsey's eyes didn't try to stay open. Betsey's eyes lowered and words she'd heard from Vida somehow strayed from her lips: "I think that might be a bit forward, Eugene." Then she stood glowing right next to him, so the hem of her dress danced along his back. "Maybe if you were to come calling again, I might see things differently."

Betsey was thinking now on what she'd heard Liliana and Mavis discussing. Some "she" out there getting it or giving it to Eugene Boyd himself. No. He could wait till some other time. She needed to know if he was serious; besides, Vida had come out on the porch to crochet with the sunset and to make sure this darned boy went on his way.

"Grandma, this is Eugene Boyd. He's a friend of Charlie's."

Vida began her crocheting, some afghan for one of her daughters, swinging in the rocker reserved for her. "I suppose that's why you've got your Sunday dress on and Charlie's gone to the store. Good Evening, young man. Boyd. Seems like I've heard that name before."

"Yes, Grandma. Eugene plays ball for Soldan."

"No, that's not what I mean. I mean I think there's some Boyds from Columbia, or maybe they were from Charlotte. Carolinians, ya know."

"No, M'am. My folks are from Mississippi."

"Oh, what a shame. I thought you might be a Boyd."

Betsey and Eugene looked at each other, eyes twinkling, but fully aware they'd had their time for the day. Eugene teasingly dribbled the ball to Betsey, who took it up in rhythm. After all, she was Charlie's cousin.

"Good evening, M'am. It was nice to meet you." Eugene waved to Vida, who looked up, nodded, and went right on crocheting. Then Eugene turned to Betsey and whispered, "Maybe next time you're up in your tree, you'll be thinking on me." He pecked her on the cheek. "See ya."

Eugene began to walk on down the street, but turned round to shout, "See ya soon, Elizabeth Brown."

Betsey watched her new friend till he was completely out of sight.

"You gointa turn into a statue, if ya stay there much longer," Vida chided.

"Oh Grandma, you don't understand."

"That's what you think. Now you go on and get out of that dress before your mama wakes up and finds out you've been entertaining on the street."

"Oh Grandma, I was not. He came to see Charlie."

"Charlie's not here, Betsey. Anybody could tell you that. So if the boy came to see Charlie, why was he so busy talking to you? You don't look like Charlie. So don't call something what it's not. That little fresh boy came by here to see you."

"Grandma, that's just not true."

"That dress does more telling than your mouth'll ever do. Now, get on with ya. I mean to tell your mother to give you a good talking to. Now these boys gointa come creeping around. There's only so much a girl can do."

"Grandma, stop. Why do you have to say something to Mama. We were sitting here talking, that's all."

"That's all for now. A girl's got to think on her future."

"Think on my future? Grandma, that's such a long way off. Let's think on right now. I'm gonna change my clothes and you won't say anything to Mama, okay?"

"If ya get a move on maybe, maybe not."

Betsey moved as elegantly as she knew how up the front porch, past her grandmother, past the cut glass in the front door, and up the same stairs she'd glided down to meet Eugene Boyd. In her room she laid her dress out as if it were covered with emeralds and pearls, diamonds and things. She might actully have a beau. Maybe Grandma was right, and Eugene Boyd had set his sights on little Miss Betsey Brown.

Jane rolled over in her bed. She'd spent most of the day putting her house back in order, missed work, missed her husband, missed her dreams of quiet and luxury, missed her version of mothering. Why do they have to be so much trouble? Why can't they just act right? Why aren't they lined up at the door in the morning all clean and silent. Oh silence. What she would give for an hour's silence. Greer would never understand. He *liked* noise. That's why he woke the house up with conga drums every morning. Tito Puente every evening for dinner music. Lee Morgan way into the night. No one in her house valued peace. Jane'd sent Charlie to the store for some Hershey's chocolates, where was he? Why did that boy always take twice as long to do a thing as anybody else would. There was nobody else she could depend on, besides Betsey.

"Elizabeth, come see your mother," Jane called down the hall. Betsey was lying next to her dress, imagining herself cheering for Eugene at the basketball game and then going to Mr. Robinson's where everybody could see them.

"What, Mama?" she whispered.

"Elizabeth, are you up here? Come into my room. I want to talk to you."

Of all the times to want to talk this was not one of them. Betsey'd been kissed. She didn't want to talk, she wanted to hold her mouth still just like when Eugene had kissed her. It was amazing that Grandma could have figured out what had been going on. Amazing how anyone sides Betsey and Eugene existed at all. Betsey wondered if Jane had felt her kissing and that's why she wanted to talk. Jane might have sensed it through the walls or the open windows, where the scents of dusk lingered and the laughter of the little children wrapped the screens in tinkling, bubbling surprises. Betsey ran her finger along the rim of her mouth to make sure it was there, right there that Eugene had kissed her. Kiss. She wanted to know more about kissing.

"Elizabeth, do you hear me? Come to my room right now. I want to tell you something."

Jane had no idea Betsey had done anything besides study her lessons and play rope or read like she usually did. Jane noticed a soft blush in her daughter's cheeks, but beyond that she saw a little girl with magic eyes and an impish smile that was hiding some huge secret.

"Elizabeth, what are you smiling about?"

"Oh, I'm just happy, Mama, that's all. I had a wonderful day. An absolutely wonderful day."

"Well, what happened?"

"Oh, nothing. Charlie and a friend of his came over to play ball. I talked to Grandma. And it was just wonderful. That's all."

Jane motioned for Betsey to sit by her on the bed.

"Betsey, sweetheart, we're going to have to try really hard to keep the house straight and the children off your grandma's nerves until I can find someone to help out around here. I'm going to put an ad in the *St. Louis Argus* asking for someone who's good with children and can do light housework. I won't be accepting anybody off the streets again."

Betsey sank into her mother's arms. It hadn't been sucha wonderful day after all. There was good in it, like a kiss, and bad in it, like where was Miss Calhoun?

FIVE

Then Regina came. Greer'd discovered that Mr. Johnson had a granddaughter who had finished high school and was in need of a job. Jane didn't take to the notion at first. She had had her fill of the Johnsons in more ways than one, but Regina seemed to be a nice girl. Fresh, and neat, slender with a heavy curl cross her forehead, the fashion of the day. The only thing that bothered Jane was that the beautician who did Regina's hair had used an electric razor on her neck. Jane believed in the use of scissors on a woman's head, no razors. That was too common. Other than that, Regina fit right in. She sang with the children and somehow managed to keep them out of trouble.

Charlie was moon-eyed all the time. Regina wasn't that much older than he was. She was so grown though. She wore tight skirts even when she was cleaning the kitchen table legs. Her blouses pointed out straight in front of her like the Playtex bra ads said they would if you wanted "lift." Charlie's crush on Regina calmed the house considerably. He was willing to do anything she asked him to.

Betsey liked Regina cause she knew about boys. Regina wore a big gold ring from Roscoe round her neck, on a gold chain that danced in the cleavage of her breasts every time she bent down. Every afternoon after school Regina read out loud to Margot and Sharon and Betsey from *True Romance* and *Love Is the Way*. The girls would huddle round Regina, whose left ankle was decorated with a bracelet that had a heart with an arrow going through the center. Regina wore hose with a seam down the back and was always pushing her cuticles back or using emery boards to save her nails.

Regina liked the way Jane lived, even if Jane had second thoughts about it herself. A doctor, a big house, a bunch of children, a garden and porches everywhere you looked. Regina sometimes took the girls upstairs to Jane's room to try on Jane's evening gowns. Jane entertained a lot. That's how the children knew about the rhumba, chocolate-covered grasshoppers, and caviar. Regina and the girls played dress-up till it was time for Regina to get dinner started, or till Vida came ambling along, humming a song to let everyone know she was in the general vicinity.

Vida believed deep in her soul that Regina was a bad influence on the girls at this critical stage of their lives. Rouged cheeks on weekdays and lipstick at 8:00 in the morning were not signs of careful living, to Vida's mind. So much preening in all the mirrors, from Sharon on up, caused Vida to click her teeth and shake her head. Jane didn't understand young folks was the decision Vida reached. If Jane understood young folks, she'd know that Regina was introducing the girls, and that ruffian Charlie, to more than orderly living. Regina carried the children all around the town, every time one of those colored singers with straightened hair like a white woman's came to town. Why, once the girls did a whole routine from somebody called Mary Wells or Baby Washington. Something about "Bells." The problem was not that Regina didn't have a hold on the household, but that she had too much a hold on the children. They quoted everything she said, and Regina was hardly more than a child herself, all dolled up in jewelry and perfumes.

Where Regina came from the curtains in the windows hung limp from heat and lack of care, and it wasn't unheard of for youngsters to rear children of their own. The Johnsons lived over by St. Mary's Hospital, that's how Greer had met them, clinic patients. Every one of the Johnsons had something wrong with them. Something that came from too little of everything. Not enough food, not enough exercise, not enough light, not enough love. Got to the point that old man Johnson most gave up, that's why Greer invested so much time and energy with them. He couldn't stand the idea of losing another colored family to the pressure, not just high blood pressure but the pressure of little rooms smelling of too many people and little wants feeding big hungers for light and air. Stairs had to smell of more than oldness and urine. There was a way to raise a girl to be a lady who was not a lady of the night. Greer'd made the Johnsons his special project, despite Vida's complaints that Regina was bringing what she came from to where it didn't belong, the ears and imaginations of her grandchildren. Even Charlie, who should have known better, was walking like he belonged to one of those bunches of bad boys, wielding knives and pipes in the alleys that made the not so grand thoroughfares of St. Louis a world unto themselves.

Regina's longtime boyfriend Roscoe was studying to be a mechanic. He was going to have his own gas station one day. He'd told Regina so. He'd told all the children. Charlie couldn't stand him, his presence, or his plans for Regina.

"Yeah, I'ma get Regina a fine house and I'ma take her to New York City one day," Roscoe boasted. He was a chunky, good-natured, muscular guy with a short neck and straight back. His hands were rough, but he whittled the grease out of his nails each evening. He thought on the colors of his gas station, Regina opening the door for him each day with an apron on, a kiss and hug good-bye. Sometimes Roscoe would get a little edgy, wondering if he could manage to support a wife and get a business started at the same time. Sometimes he thought he wanted to see the world before it all got away from him, but in high school he'd promised Regina his heart and a way out of her grandfather's house.

When Vida napped and the children were off at play or at school, all that autumn Roscoe whistled up to Regina's room. She'd come on down and hot kisses in each other's arms and rolls and grabs wheeled them bout the yard. Regina enjoyed Roscoe's visits. She imagined she was Jane and her husband was home for some loving. Regina took no mind of her body when she was with him. Her woman gave into his man and there was a hush, subduing her throbs and moans in the midst of a sepia rush that was Roscoe. Mrs. Brown had told her specifically, "No callers," but Roscoe wasn't a caller. He was the world, her future.

"I'ma wear your kisses round my neck. I'ma feel your hands up and down my spine. They gonna say 'there's Roscoe's gal' and they won't be lying. I'ma swing my hips with this gold round my ankles. They gonna say 'ever since that Roscoe got holdt to that gal aint no man could handle her sweet sweet meat."

Roscoe and Regina hadn't spied Betsey and the girls peering through the bushes.

"Are you gonna kiss her now, Roscoe?" Betsey pleaded.

"Betsey, this aint none of your business!"

Regina tried to get herself back in some order, but it was no use. They'd seen too much already.

"I could kiss her now. Couldn't I, Regina?"

Roscoe lifted Regina off the grass and into the air, sliding her down his body like a man who didn't give a damn what the world thought.

"Betsey, you know your mama won't approve."

"Please, Gina, a real kiss. I just love kisses."

Charlie shouted from the back porch, "He don't have no business round here. Regina don't need to be kissing nobody."

Regina turned round, waved Charlie off her mind. "Charlie, you mind your business and I'll tend to mine."

The girls egged Regina and Roscoe on, as they came up onto the porch.

"Please, a kiss. A real kiss."

"I'll give you a kiss, Betsey," Charlie offered sarcastically.

"Charlie, go on away, will you? Don't nobody want no kisses from you."

That was exactly what Charlie was thinking. It made him mad. He'd fix em. He'd fix all of em.

Margot and Sharon took up for Betsey, who was thinking on Eugene, of course.

"You her cousin, simple."

"She wouldn't want no kiss from you."

Betsey tried to explain it wasn't that she wanted a kiss. She did want a kiss, but not that kind of kiss. Roscoe and Regina had graduated kissing to an art. Betsey knew beginning kisses, but she wanted big ones, like when you fall in love. Roscoe and Regina were in love. Love kisses were the best kind. There was no denying that a kiss from someone you loved was different from any other kind of kiss and should be studied up on and looked at carefully, so you could recognize it when love came down on you. That's what love did. It came down on you like rain or sunshine. All of a sudden there'd be this sensation in all the muscles and a dizziness in your head and a reaching out for someone and love'd be all on you. That's the kind of kiss Betsey wanted to see. True romance.

"I wanna see a kiss like when you fall in love."

"You aint never been in love," Charlie retorted.

"Of course not, I'm getting ready though," Betsey flew right back at him. She was determined now to get this kissing lesson.

"Mama and Daddy don't do that." Allard scrunched up his face.

"Where you think they got you at," Sharon replied.

"We don't come from no tongue kissing," Allard insisted.

"Y'all don't understand what you been missing," Betsey exclaimed. "Look at that. How can they breathe? How can they? Oh, when will I fall in love?"

"I wanna be carried off my feet." Margot pranced.

"I wanta be fainting in the street." Sharon lay on her side looking at the sky.

"I want him chasing me every heart beat." Margot couldn't stop leaping in the air.

"I bet they get germs," Allard added.

"No, Allard, people in love don't get germs," Betsey assured him.

"No. One of these days some boy from somewhere . . ."

"Hey, how bout right over here." Eugene walked up to the porch, his eyes seeing no one but Betsey.

"Well, maybe someday some boy from somewhere'll come over to share all my grown-up ways, cause I'ma be a woman someday."

Just as Eugene was about to let Betsey have her wish, Charlie came out from the kitchen with Vida by his side. Regina didn't have a minute to let go of Roscoe before Vida began her harangue.

"You know, I can't seem to find my fan. It's so hot around here these days, it's a wonder a body could stand to wear clothes, much less be all on top of another body in all this heat."

Regina pulled away from Roscoe and tried to stand up tall so all the wrinkles in her blouse might straighten out and the passion in her cheeks somehow simmer down. Yet Vida went on in a circle around them, looking so close at the damp and rumpled couple.

"Don't you think it's much too terribly warm, Regina, to be receiving company? The chirren are beside themselves in all this heat. My, my, here's my fan in my pocket. And who might be this young man? On his way back to work somewhere, no doubt."

"Mrs. Murray, this is Roscoe, my beau."

"You don't say, Regina. Allard seems a mite untidy and the girls could use some talcum quite nicely. If you don't mind, I'll see your visitor to the door. Then you and I will talk."

Roscoe stepped up to Vida. "I didn't mean no harm, M'am. It's just that she's my gal and I missed her so . . ."

"Regina is off on Sunday, young man, not Tuesday, not Wednesday or Thursday or Friday." Vida ended that.

Roscoe defended himself anyhow. "My intentions are honorable, M'am."

"No need to impress me, young man. I've got no high-school drop-out to fend for. I'd hoped Regina would elevate or gravitate to her potential, but it seems her bodily needs are more the essence of her background."

"This young man is worth more than you know, Mrs. Murray." Regina intercepted what looked like an ugly fight. "I've got plans of my own with this one. I'ma make me a home with younguns of my own who'll beat the living shit out of the likes of you and your kind."

"That's quite enough, Regina."

"Oh no, that aint enough! You all in a tizzy cause the chirren asked us what love is. I can't work in no house where you got to run round like a mouse cause you in love. I'll be leaving this afternoon."

"That won't be soon enough to suit me, my dear." And Vida marched back off into the house.

Roscoe took Regina's face up in his hands. "When there's enough, we won't have to take low to her kind. When there's enough, nobody'll look down on me and mine." And he rocked her till the salty brine of Vida's words fell away.

Eugene and Betsey were by each other's side. Eugene took Betsey's hand. "When there's enough, you go where you have to go and give what you got. When you're really in love, there's never enough to go round.

Betsey was afraid. Being in love brought the wrath of her grandma on Regina's head. Lord knows what would happen to her if she were to fall in love, too. Eugene wouldn't let her go, though. He kept whispering, "When you're really in love, there's never enough to go round." Betsey's heart began to beat less from fear than from anticipation. Eugene and Betsey were at a new stage. Betsey was over her head. Eugene, clicking his heels.

Regina kissed each of the children and hugged them all together, like a litter of kittens. Roscoe took her off and all Betsey could think to say was: "Look, they're in love." Looking at Eugene she wondered did they look like that, too, but there wasn't much time to ponder. Vida's voice pierced their ears: "Betsey Brown, you bring yourself and all the rest of those chirren in here right this minute. You hear me?"

Betsey was afraid again and let go of Eugene's hands.

"Come on y'all, we're in for it now. It's all Charlie's fault. Getting Grandma, when he knew we were having a kissing lesson."

Charlie was beginning to get on Betsey's nerves, especially

when she saw that Vida'd made him a glass of iced tea, when he was the one she swore was no good northern trash.

"I want all of you to sit at this table and listen to every word I have to say. Y'all were mighty impressed with some low-down niggah mess."

Betsey kicked Charlie's leg under the table. "Why'd you do it, Charlie? You knew what would happen."

"She wasn't 'sposed to be keeping company on Aunt Jane's time. Sides that, she was a little tramp."

"You hush your mouth, Charles, I'm talking now. Get that gal off your minds. This is the last time for such carrying on. Lord, I need my fan to soothe my soul. My children been exposed to Satanic ways. Lord, protect these girls. Keep those panties up and them legs closed. Lord, Lord, keep those fresh boys out these fresh girls' pants. Betsey, you mind that Boyd boy, ya hear. Oh, Jesus, you know I need my fan."

"Grandma, Regina's in love. That's all."

"Elizabeth Brown, taking up with trash is gointa be your undoing. Now go study your lessons like you had some sense."

"That's right, Elizabeth, go study your lessons and stay way from trash, ya hear," Charlie echoed, so satisfied.

Betsey walked away from the table, hating Charlie for making Regina little in everybody's mind, when each of them knew he was the one had a thing for her. Betsey kept hearing Eugene say, "When you're really in love, there's never enough." Maybe that was why her mother and father went off so much. There were only two of them and five of the children plus Grandma, that made six. So their love got all divided up into little pieces among the whole family. But Betsey knew her mama and papa were really in love cause they'd said so, and though they'd never kissed like Roscoe and Regina they kissed in some kinda way. Betsey could tell by her mama's eyes and her papa's easy grin. What she didn't know and wanted very much to understand was why if you're really in love there's never enough. It seemed to her if you were really in love there would be more than you needed.

Jane couldn't believe her ears. Regina gone at a time like this. Not now, when the white folks were going to follow the law instead of taking the laws. Not now, Regina couldn't be gone. But she was. So much the better, Vida thought. Teaching those chirren all that nasty business. Best be rid of dirt fore it gets under your nails, was her way of thinking. But now, with the buses and the new schools, God only knew what miseries her children would have to endure with all those peckerwoods out there. Jane was disheartened. She felt a collapsing of her spirit akin to despair. She had no idea where half these places the children were going to go to school were, much less how to get them there. Would there be ugly crowds of thin-lipped rednecks throwing tomatoes and bottles at her children? Would she have to go up to the school every day on account of some poor racist child who didn't know niggah is not the same as Negro? What was going to happen to her children now the white folks put their minds on integrating some things. Jane didn't miss white folks, she didn't like white folks, she tried not to think about them. She kept her world as colored as she could. There was enough of it. From Langston Hughes to Sojourner Truth, her children's worlds were hardly deprived.

What on earth was she to do? She could refuse to let her children be bused. She could put them in the Catholic school.

If she got mad enough she could keep them home and teach them herself, but then how could they pay the mortgage? Jane's head was buzzing frantically, when Greer brought her a deck of cards and a highball.

"They're going."

"Greer, how can you say that? They're babies. Who knows what those crackers'll do to them. I just don't know."

"They're paving the way for those yet to come, Jane. There's thousands of lives that depend on our children having the courage to go somewhere they've never been accepted, or wanted, when they have a right to go and a right to the best education our taxes pay for."

Jane took the deck of cards and mechanically dealt herself a hand of bridge. She played every hand. Greer listened to Miles Davis and Art Blakey, while his wife, who'd been round white folks all her life, decided her children's futures.

Hesitantly, but ever so seriously, Jane spoke.

"All right. They can go, but at the first sign of trouble of any kind, they go to the Catholic school . . . is that understood?"

Greer nodded yes, and the two of them were quiet together, praying no one of theirs would be hurt or pierced to the quick by some flying words outta peckerwood mouths. Jane and Greer knew about these things. They'd been chastened since birth by the scorn and violence the race had known. They'd been brought up on lynchings and riots, name-calling and "No Colored Allowed." The neighborhood had saved them, they thought. With the Negro-owned businesses, the hairdressers and laundry, the school teachers and the shadows of the great trees, the neighborhood had sheltered them from what they knew was on the outside: the white people.

All the usual commotion of an ordinary evening in the Brown house was stilled. Even Charlie wasn't bad-mouthing the girls or telling tales of his exploits. Margot and Sharon weren't playing make-believe. Betsey wasn't reading about anything. The children knew the morning brought a new way of living, another realm into their lives, one they'd been taught was dangerous and hostile. The white people. A classroom full of white people. No Twandas, Veejays, and Charlotte Anns. No Willettas and the rivalries tween Sumner and Soldan. Nothing familiar. Maybe not even any dill pickles wrapped in brown paper or candies like Mr. Robinson's. What could you talk about with them? What would they want to talk about? What they knew awready was shouts, bottles, and catsup. This no one mentioned out loud. Only Allard crawled on his bed crying: "I don't want to go. I don't want to go off with no white folks. They gonna kill me. Mama, they gonna kill me."

Jane reassured her babies as best she could. Greer let everyone play the conga drums, but they all knew their lives would never be the same. Betsey couldn't understand why they weren't good enough already. Why did she have to take three different buses to learn the same things with white children that she'd been learning with colored children? How was she going to keep her friends if she never saw them? Why didn't the white children come to her school? Let *them* get up at dawn and take a trillion different trolleys. Why did the Negroes have to do everything the hard way? Why weren't they good enough already?

Jane prayed through her sleep. Greer did his best to quiet

her fears, the anxious look in her eyes, how her limbs crouched beneath his, taut, ready to run.

Betsey slipped from her bed to her window. Through her tree she could see the stars and clouds that were so lithe the moon shone through them. She wondered if the white children saw things like that. Did they search the skies at night for beauty and answers to wishes? The darkness was a comfort to her. The window slid open without so much as a creak. Betsey went over to the tree limb that was toughest, the one that could hold all her weight, grabbed hold and pulled herself up. This was one night she would see all the stars and the moon as the sun rose, when there was that peculiar mingling of past and tomorrows, when the sun glanced cross the sky to the moon hoverin over the telephone wires, and everyone else was ignorant of the powers of light and the dark.

SIX

Jane had never been in and out of the refrigerator so much in her life. Nobody wanted anything they usually ate.

"I never eat baloney, Mama," Margot pouted.

"I do, I eat it all the time," Allard said.

"Y'all shut up, and get out my way. I've got to see if my bus is coming." Sharon pushed her way to the window, paper bag lunch in hand.

"You in that much of a hurry for the crackers to spit on you?" Charlie asked.

"But, Mama, I don't like tuna." Margot still hadn't found a

luncheon meat that satisfied her tastes. "I don't want cheese, either."

Betsey was roaming among them like a prelate. "It's the law. Integration is the law."

Jane reached her limit.

"This is it. Here are your lunches. It's the law. Go to your bus stops and have a good day."

Greer lifted Allard off the floor to the ceiling and let him play Spiderman. Allard was frightened, one could tell by the solemn gleam in his eyes.

"Come on, Allard. We don't want the white folks to say that a gifted colored child was late, now do we?"

"Daddy, do I have to go? I don't want to go!"

Vida wasn't much help. She cleaned behind Jane, who was folding the lunch bags, muttering, "I don't understand this. I just don't understand this."

"Daddy, I am not colored. I am a Negro," Allard announced while clinging to the ceiling.

"That's my boy. That's exactly what you tell them, too." Greer chuckled.

Vida kept on, "I don't know why they have to go to the white folks' school. I just don't understand."

Greer patted Vida on her shoulders, sighing, "It's the law, Mama. Remember, I told you separate and equal was not separate and equal, just separate? Remember that?"

Jane looked at every one of her youngsters. Were they all ready? Did they look nice and clean and just like she wanted to remember them? She mustn't think like that. Nothing was going to happen.

"Mama, my shirt don't fit." Allard fidgeted.

"Your shirt doesn't fit," Jane said.

"No. It don't."

"No, it doesn't," Betsey chimed.

"That's what I *said,*" Allard answered, indignant.

"Why does my child have to live round all these niggahs and talk so low?" Vida asked Jane in her most sincere voice.

"Mama, he's on his way right now to a white school." Jane was getting mad with everybody.

"But he talks like a niggah."

"Allard, you must be the niggah them white folks talk about. Grandma says you sound like one. Pickaninny. Blackie. Boot."

"Charlie, you shut up. You're going to scare Allard to death." Jane was ready for them to go now.

"I was just practicing, Aunt Jane. I was preparing Allard for what's coming round the corner."

"All that's coming round the corner is the bus, Charlie. Stop filling the children's minds with mess."

"Aunt Jane, it's not mess. Look at all these colored children being an experiment. What do you think those white folks gonna say? We aint nothing permanent. Niggahs come and go and die. Emmett Till was my age, Aunt Jane."

"That's enough, Charlie. The Lord will see us through all this."

"But Aunt Jane, you think they're gonna pass us by, cause Betsey's gifted or Allard's so smart, or Sharon's only so dark? You think we can't be lynched? You think they don't see us for who we are? That's being fool—"

"Hush up that nonsense, you hoodlum northern trash," Vida interrupted.

"Mama, please don't say that. The children are agitated, that's all." Jane pulled her hands through her hair which was dampened with tears and sweat she'd been pushing up her forehead.

"Greer, let's go. Please, can we go?"

"The children don't seem so organized, Jane."

"Dammit, Greer, between you, the Supreme Court, the buses and the boys, I think I might die. I swear, I think I just might die."

Charlie leaned over to Allard, whispering, "We gonna get some white tail and say we did it for Emmett Till."

"Tail, I don't want any tail, Charlie."

"Hush your filthy mouth, you hear me? Hush!" Vida shouted.

Janc pulled Greer close to her. "Let's get out of here." As she went out the door, Jane turned and waved kisses back to her children. She wept on Greer's shoulder all the way to work.

Vida watched the children line up, military style, to go to their individual bus stops. She shook her head as the chant she heard them shouting reached into the quiet of the house.

"All they can say is it's the law
All they can say is it's the law
Do they do it? Do they do it?
Naw."

Then Charlie's voice saying: "Does a peckerwood hit you in the head during math?" Margot echoing, "Do the police watch you count your own money at the store?" Then Betsey adding, "Do white boys pull up your dress to see a niggah's behind?"

"No, not to see your behind. To see if you got a tail," Charlie answered. "It's the law and it's a mess. Hey, we gonna miss our buses," Charlie cried, alarmed.

"So what?" Betsey shouted for the whole neighborhood to hear: "We misst our buses. Who would give a damn? White folks wish our feet didn't even touch their holy ground. So what, we miss our buses? Who you think gonna come, Eisenhower, Faubus? Po' white trash with guns gonna escort us to our classes and make us eat the flag, while they tell us how slavery really wasn't quite so bad."

Off they went, belligerent, afraid and feeling totally put upon.

The brigade scattered at Union Boulevard.

"I get the number four."

"I'm catching the twelve."

"I'm heading southwest."

"I don't wanta go," Allard pleaded.

"So what niggah? It's the law." That's all Charlie had to say. And they went their separate ways.

Vida wandered round the house picking up this and that: a ribbon, a crayon, a dustball. They got some nerve, those foolish urchins. They've got the honor of being Americans. They free and smart. They got good blood. And all they got on their minds is how it was in slavery times, as if we came from slaves. What a mess they've made of our genealogy, everybody knows we were freedmen. Then Vida stopped that train of thought, cause in order to be a freedman somebody would have had to be a slave and that concept did not compute.

When Betsey got to her new school, it loomed like a granite tomb over her head. Nobody spoke to her, so she didn't speak to them. It was like they were all dead. The white children weren't dirty or anything. They didn't even have red necks as far as she could tell, but they didn't smile at her the way she was usedta Susan Linda grinning at the corner of the schoolyard. This time Betsey had the whole corner to herself. Wherever she stepped, the other children found somewhere else to go. It was the first time Betsey knew she was someplace, yet felt no evidence of it. Maybe they couldn't see her. No, Betsey knew better than that. They chose not to, like the color of her skin was a blight. Betsey wisht it would rub off. She'd rub coloredness all over the damn place. Then where would they go to get away from the niggahs?

Mrs. Leon was the first person to address her by her name, Elizabeth Brown. In a linen suit and a tailored blouse with a blue bow at the collar, Mrs. Leon looked like a big little girl to Betsey. But at least Mrs. Leon didn't seem to think there was anything strange about her.

"Class, this is our new pupil, Betsey, I think she likes to be called. Is that right?"

"Yes, M'am."

"Well, you have a seat behind Jan there at the right, and we'll start our geography lessons. All your books should be in your desk. Let me know if you are missing anything." Mrs. Leon smiled.

Betsey thought maybe Mrs. Leon wasn't white at all, maybe she was passing, like in that book *Imitation of Life*. Or maybe she was what Jane called "well-meaning white people." At any rate Mrs. Leon broke the ice and the thrill of a new place and new faces came over Betsey as easily as the shadows had blackened her path.

It was luck or planning on Mrs. Leon's part, but the geography lesson had all to do with Africa. Greer had insisted that his children know every emerging African state's name and location, so Betsey was soaring with information. It turned out that the children didn't hate her actually, they just didn't know what to do with her. They'd never seen colored who didn't work for them or playing in some part of town nobody wanted to live in. But as the words Ghana, Nigeria, Sierra Leone, and Senegal rolled off Betsey's tongue, they sounded as romantic and elegant as France, Germany, Alsace-Lorraine, or Bulgaria. Nobody could sing the words to "Rockin' Robin" at recess, but they played hop-scotch the same. One girl with wavy blond hair kept kosher, which Betsey didn't understand. She'd ask Jane. Another girl with brown hair and blue-green eyes, Randa, asked if Betsey would show her how to jump double-dutch. Betsey did her best, but the rhythm just wasn't coming from the rope-twirlers. Then the bell rang.

Betsey went back to Mrs. Leon with hopes things might get even better. The children who stayed away from her were as unswerving in their obstinance as Betsey was becoming optimistic about her new experience. Would she become one of them? Betsey often thought Susan Linda was most colored, cause she was too poor to be really white. There was the possibility of them rubbing off on her instead of her rubbing off on them. A fast trip to the girls' lavatory relieved Betsey of that dilemma. She'd go home just as brown as she'd arrived. Everybody at home would recognize her. No two ways about it. She was still Betsey Brown.

But the new school, Dewey School, would never be like her real school. It wasn't till the bus eased up Delmar Boulevard and the colored people were going on about their business, carrying things from the dry cleaners, going up the stairs to their apartments or the beauty shops, lingering by the corners exchanging tales, waiting in line for fried fish or shrimp, slinging barbeque sauce over ribs and burgers, playing honest-to-God double-dutch and liking it, that Betsey felt like she was at home. When she got off the streetcar Veejay and Eugene were waiting for her.

"Girl, we been here for three trolleys. How far is that place?"

"Oh Veejay, I'm so glad to see you." Betsey hugged her lost friend for dear life. It was so good to be around her own kind, friends who understood her already. Eugene was pleased nothing had happened to disturb his girl. Mr. Robinson served them all chocolate sundaes with cherries and teeny nuts all the way around.

"You made a step forward for the race today, Betsey. I'm real proud of you." Mr. Robinson knew most of Betsey's comings and goings. His pharmacy was right next to the trolley stop, so if you were going somewhere Mr. Robinson knew. He also knew if you didn't go somewhere. One time Betsey'd tried to make-believe she got on the trolley to go to her piano lesson, but she just stood at the door and then jumped off. She stayed the whole time in the store with Mr. Robinson and then tried to walk home as if she'd been to her lesson with that fat old Mr. Benjamin who had nine children and a wife who sang opera. But Mr. Robinson had already called her parents to say she was staying in the pharmacy an awfully long time.

Jane let Betsey go on about the Benjamin children and their

West Indian accents, how well she was doing with her scales and the new Chopin piece, when Greer mentioned casually that Mr. Robinson had said what good company she'd been all afternoon, business was kind of slow, Betsey was a wonderful child to talk to. What a licking that led to. So Betsey never tried to do anything in front of Mr. Robinson anymore. He stuck with the grown-ups, but today he was proud of her. Maybe he'd call Jane and Greer and tell them that, too.

Eugene walked Betsey home after they'd walked Veejay round to Charlotte Ann's where she was visiting till her mother got off work.

"I can't wait for you every day, Betsey. I've got practice, but I was worried today. What with all them white people. Never know what they'll do."

"They weren't nearly as bad as I thought they'd be, Eugene. Honest. Why I even made one friend, Randa. But they're not like us. That's the truth. They can't dance or play rope. They don't talk the same. It's almost like going to another country."

"Well, you be sure and tell me if one of those white boys messes with you, you hear?"

"Uh huh. I'll tell you." Betsey wanted to throw her arms round Eugene's neck and kiss him a Roscoe and Regina kiss for saying what he'd just said. He was willing to protect her. He wanted to know if anything happened to her. She held herself back, smiling from one braid to the other.

"Eugene, I'm really glad you like me that much."

Eugene blushed a bit and was on his way. Betsey didn't know from day to day when she'd see him, but she knew he was there if she needed him.

The children's commutes put the dinner back by an hour

and a half. Jane and Greer were home before everybody except Allard, who kept exclaiming: "Mama, they didn't kill me. Look, Mama, I'm alive."

"Yes, you are, Allard. You are very much alive. I told you not all the white people were evil. There's evil in every group."

"Yeah, Charlie's evil."

"No, Charlie isn't evil. He's having growing pains, that's all."

"Look, Daddy, I'm alive. The white folks didn't kill me."

Margot and Sharon luckily had each other for support at their school, where nothing in particular happened. They were just dirty and fuzzy-headed enough to let Jane know they'd spent their time playing and were out of danger. The missing Charlie changed the scene entirely, when he walked in with a torn shirt and a black eye. Everybody ran up to him. Vida went to get a piece of cold beef to put over that eye. Jane hugged him as she loosened the remnants of the pressed shirt from her nephew's back.

"Those dirty guineas callt me a niggah, Uncle Greer. They callt me a niggah. I didn't have any choice. I had to defend myself."

"All you could think to do is use your hands, Charles. Is that all you've learned? Fighting white folks won't change their minds. It just makes them meaner. Now you sit down and let's take a look at what's happened to you. How many were there, Charlie?" Greer asked, quite serious.

"Five greasy-headed wop bastards."

"Charlie, you didn't learn that language here, and I won't have it in my house." Jane was exasperated. Of all the children she'd been worried about, Charlie was the last one she thought would have trouble. It was his temper. No. That was a lie. It was the white people. No. It was Greer filling the children's heads with stories of heroes and standing up for yourself at any cost. Jane didn't know what to do but soothe the aching bones of her sister's son and listen.

"Why didn't you get the principal or the school guard, Charles?" Greer went on.

"What for? So they could all gang up on me? I'm not going back there."

"Yes you are. What's the point of having stood up for yourself if you're going to back down your next move."

Greer was thinking maybe he should have taken each of the children to school himself. That way everybody would know that there was somebody to be reckoned with if so much as a hair on the head of a Brown was put out of place. Jane didn't quite know how to handle this. She'd promised Catholic schools at the first sign of trouble, but she and Greer also had a pact, which was not to contradict each other in front of the children.

"But Uncle Greer, there's more of them than there are of me. I'm gonna carry me some of my fellas back over there. Let them see what a pack of 'niggahs' can do to their greasy-just-off-the-boat asses."

"Charles, I did say that was quite enough of that language. The other children don't need to hear you talking like that. It won't help anything."

"Look, Charlie, the guineas didn't kill me either," Allard jumped in.

"See what I mean, Charles, you've got to be careful what you say."

When Vida returned with the meat for Charlie's eye, she chirped: "See, there's no sense going where you're not wanted. White folks are enough trouble far off, no need to be all up under them too." With that Vida set the little steak on Charlie's face and examined the bruises on his chest.

"Looks just like when they pulled my great-uncle Julius out his house to lynch him. That's what it looks like." Vida just shook her head.

Jane looked up, startled. "Mama, you weren't even alive when that happened."

"There's some things you never forget, Jane. It runs in you blood memory. That's what it does."

"Oh, Mama."

"Charlie, tomorrow you and I will be going to that school together. We'll see who wants to take on the Golden Gloves Champion of 1941 and the latest hero of the race."

"Really, Uncle Greer? You'll go there with me? I don't want it to look like you're seeing to a little guy like Allard or nothing."

"No, we'll go, two men together."

"Y'all best leave those white folks alone." Vida slipped away to the yard where there were only green things. They understood her ways of thinking. Grow in your own patch. Stay put and blossom.

Jane suddenly realized there was no dinner ready. She left the family staring at Charlie, while Greer tried to make the best of it, boosting the spirits of the new pioneers with the family chant, "The work of the Negro is never done."

Yet Charlie's bruises brought home what they'd all been worried about. The vengeance of the white people. It could have been any one of them, Mrs. Leon or no Mrs. Leon. Were there enough "well-meaning white folks" to outdo the ordinary ones who'd attack a boy like Charlie five to one?

Betsey counted her blessings. She looked at her sisters and Allard, grateful no harm had befallen them. She thought not being spoken to was the kindness of the Lord compared to what Charlie'd faced. But now there was the issue of safety. Daddy couldn't be everywhere with everyone every day. Somebody had to earn a living. It was clear to Betsey the police weren't earning theirs.

"Girls, come help me with the supper," Jane shouted from the kitchen.

"All right, Mama," but none of them moved. They were waiting for some sign from Charlie that everything was all right again.

"You heard Aunt Jane, go get dinner ready, would you? I'm hungry."

Charlie could talk fine, but his words were slurred cause he wanted to cry too. He couldn't bear the burden of the whole race all by himself. Not every day. Alone. He was so glad Uncle Greer had decided to go with him just once. He'd let those guineas, oh, those people, know he wasn't alone in this. Not by a long shot.

Vida'd come in from her garden and run everybody, including Jane, out of the kitchen. She said there was too much mess going on in the house, and cooking gave her peace of mind. The children needed to do their lessons, so the white folks would know they weren't any dummies.

"Look, Grandma, the white folks didn't kill me."

"Of course not, Allard. They only kill little boys who don't mind."

"Mama! That was an inappropriate answer," Jane said, irritated.

"Well, I told him what I think."

"Allard, the white people aren't going to kill anybody. What happened to Charlie happens everywhere, even between Negroes themselves. Remember what I told you: there's evil folks in every walk of life. Their color has nothing to do with it."

"That's not what Charlie said. He said there was five of them and one of him."

"Allard, Charlie's mad right now. Everything he says when he's mad isn't true."

"No, I saw it. He's got a black eye."

"Mama, you know those white boys beat on Charlie," Sharon added adamantly.

"See what I told you bout messing with them white folks." Vida was sprinkling the greens with cayenne, thinking maybe she ought to give each of the children a little bit to throw on the whites who bothered them.

"Mama, this is not the time to discourage them."

"I'm not discouraging them. I'm encouraging them to mind their ways round those people."

"They are not 'those people,' they are just some other people. Mama, please, let's not argue."

"Well, if they bother me, I'm gonna set em on fire, that's what I'm gointa do," Allard declared.

"You'll do no such thing."

"Yes I will. They go up in flames to glory. Won't they, Grandma?"

"I'm not sure that's where they'll go, Allard."

"Mama, how could you say such a thing when you know Allard has a predilection for fire-setting. I just can't believe it."

"Well, why don't you take a look at Charlie's eye and see what's to be believed, then?"

"Greer, Greer, take me out of here. I have to go somewhere and clear my head. Tween the white folks, Mama, the Supreme Court, the buses, the boys, the girls at that stage, oh my God, Greer, please get me out of here."

Greer stood in the doorway of the kitchen toward the back steps.

"Come on upstairs, Jane. It's quiet. I'm going to take all the children to school tomorrow, make no mistake. Right now, though, I think I better take care of you."

"I just don't know how much of this I can take," Jane murmured as she and Greer slowly walked to their room.

"It's not that bad, is it?" Greer stopped at the bend in the stairs where the children couldn't spy on them and wrapped his arms around her.

"It's not my idea of a quiet family life."

"These aren't peaceful times, Jane." Greer kissed her temple and held her face in his hand. "You're as strong as I am. We'll make it through this and we'll reminisce bout the evening you were storming about, saying you were losing your mind. The evening I asked for a little bit of loving at quarter of six."

"Now?"

"Yep."

"What about dinner and the children?"

"They'll be right there, believe me, they aren't going anywhere."

"Must be you think I'm crazy, too. All you can think I have

to do is to go off making love to you at quarter of six in the evening. I couldn't have conceived this is where we'd be thirteen years from then. And thirteen years from now?"

"We'll still be together, sweetheart. How about a tango, a bolero, a samba, a mambo?"

Jane snuggled up to Greer. "Just nothing too African, you hear. The bed can't take it."

Betsey peeked around the corner of the landing they were on before they ran off and locked their door.

"There's never enough when you're really in love, is there Mommy . . ."

SEVEN

The burnt-orange and clay dried leaves fell as quickly as the days went by, there wasn't enough time to catch up with her old playmates, not enough time to dig to China, never enough time to tell the white folks what she really felt about them, walking around like they owned the world. There was never any time to see Eugene. Basketball. Basketball. Basketball. Even Charlie didn't get to see him. Plus, she was to keep her mind on her studies, now she was competing with the white children—as if that hadn't been the case in the beginning. Who did they think she was gonna grow up and compete against,

Rodan? Grown-ups made such little sense. Why go lock yourself up in a room when there were sycamores and white oaks to nestle under. Why throw things and scream and holler on account of some white man coming to the door saying that the John Birch Society represented all Americans. Mama liketa jumped down the man's throat and Daddy wasn't too keen on the explanation of separate but equal that the tiny little white man presented from a global perspective. Daddy said the only way to really understand white folks was to listen to them.

Betsey thought she must know all about the white people by now, she listened to them all day long. Every day. Not the way a blues gets in your bones and has ya inchin along in tune to the smells and sways of a colored day, so it's pleasant and downright comforting, but the way the gnats be coming at ya at night if no one has any bug lotion. White folks got on ya like gnats. She missed everything on account of them. She thought on what she could do as hard on the white folks as they were hard on her.

She was a secret now, lying in the dirt and dry leaves out of sight of Mr. Jeff's gardening tools. That man had a way about him. If there was an empty plot of ground, he'd sure 'nough find something to plant in it. But Betsey'd planted herself in the shadow of her tree and the fragrance of earth to conjure some way back at the white folks which didn't have one iota of the ways of the Lord in it. She wasn't certain she was making a bargain with Satan, but even if she did, white folks did it all the time. Come hell or high water, Betsey was gonna do em up right, least in her neighborhood.

Everybody'd gone off to swim at the Y. Friday was the day they cleaned the pool, that's how come the colored could swim on Fridays. Betsey'd missed that cause she got home from the white school too late to take the carpool of colored children over there.

The street was vacant. Like a big old movie set. Nothing. Nobody to do a thing with. What could she do alone? Better yet, what could she do alone that could exclude the white folks, who were nowhere to be seen except in her wounds and aches of memories. Betsey decided to play hop-scotch, but she laid the hop-scotch pattern out with enough room to write "For Colored Only," "Crackers and Dogs Not Allowed," "Peckerwoods Got No Welcome Here," "Guineas Go Home." Betsey's hop-scotch was something to behold. Chalk never seemed so powerful as when it messed with white folks.

Betsey jumped all over her great design. She danced on the "No Whites" till it smudged beyond recognition. Then she wrote it over again till she was so tired she went into the house to take a nap.

The neighborhood was outraged. How in an era of desegregation and reconciliation of the races could such an ugly, hateful hop-scotch game appear on their street. Not one of the Negro families on the block admitted to having any hostile feelings toward white folks. Not a single one. Including the Browns, who were as astonished as the Blackburns and the Williamses that a prejudiced soul lived among them. Betsey volunteered to rid the street of the vile creation with a hose from round back of her house. There was no need to contaminate the minds of the young ones a moment longer. With a swoosh of water there'd be not one more unpleasantry about white folks visible on the block. But Betsey Brown had had her day, when she was in control.

But things were getting out of control for Jane and Greer. The melody of their first years together was wearing thin. Good help was hard to find. Good loving was hard to nurture, with the whole world going topsy-turvy round about you. Lean his kisses were, short her hugs. The children scrambled into their bed each morning with some new dilemma, or just a wet kiss from the wrong side of the bed. Jane took refuge in decks of cards she collected and hoarded from whoever was learning their numbers. Queens, kings, jacks, hearts, spades, diamonds, her other reality. Concentrated, ordered and private. Now when Jane was in college, she'd laughed at the girls whiling their days away in pinocle, bridge or whist. The drama of Bernhart, Holiday, and Horne held too much for her then. Yet now that was so far away, solitaire was her forte.

"Since when do you have time to go play cards at the Alley Cat Club?" Greer asked one night, while undressing.

"Since you went away . . . ," Jane sang sarcastically.

"You being funny or something?"

"I didn't know you had time to think about what I was doing with my leisure time. What little of it I've got."

"At the Alley Cat Club, there's only so much you can do."

"A club is a suit in a deck of cards."

Greer lay next to Jane on their bed, being sure not to disturb the game she'd been playing so intently. "Is that your way of calling a spade a spade?"

"Might be." Jane rolled over to run put her diaphragm in. She didn't really know why she bothered. It hadn't helped before.

"You don't need to do all that," Greer said.

"Oh no? You know what we're in store for if I don't, don't

you? There's awready four of em. Don't be a fool and make it five. I'll be just a second."

"I'm going to learn how to play cards, so I could see you sometimes." Greer spilled the deck marked with little forget-me-nots at the edge of the bed.

"I said I'd be right back, and you know I only play solitaire."

The house was bathed in Bessie Smith from a station Betsey'd found on the radio downstairs. Betsey was adorning herself with the curtains and some feathers, stalking the front room like a teenaged Shirley Temple who was colored to begin with.

"Betsey, turn that mess off and go to bed," Jane hollered down the halls. If it wasn't for Greer these children would have some sense. All that nasty colored music.

"Betsey, turn that mess off, do you hear me."

Bessie Smith went down one decibel. Jane let it pass and fell into Greer's arms.

"You really should come home more often."

They didn't bother to turn the lights out. The lights never went out at the Savoy or Birdland. Her skirts would twirl up toward the lights, the trumpets, and Cab Calloway's chants. All this was coming back to Jane, why she loved her husband and where they'd courted.

Downstairs Vida stole a lost moment for herself in the quiet of the parlor where she kept her photos of Frank and her children in their wedding gowns and graduation garb. The music Jane and Greer were moving to was inaudible to Vida, but the blues Betsey'd turned up again was athrilling Vida's china bones. She took the picture of Frank in his best suit off the wall and danced a strange little dance of "I love you, you scoundrel, you love of my life." She remembered, giggling a bit, that once she'd gone to a roadhouse and danced on a dime, somewhere near Savannah.

"Oh that Frank of mine!" fell from her lips, made her smile. "Now, I wasn't there on Sundays, hardly ever on a Monday, but I could get most every man to smile, if I did a Charleston for a while." Vida pulled up her nightie and twitched her thin legs this way and that. "I wonder was it like this?" she asked herself, "Or more like this?" Vida slipped her hips to the east and then to the west. "Oh no, I couldn't have been so bawdy, not nearly so naughty." Vida let herself down in an easy chair by the window where she watched her Frank come up the front stairs of her father's house. "I wonder if Vida is receiving company tonight?" Between the Bible and her man's photograph Vida drifted to a land of glory smitten with ragtime, her other times.

Betsey was in her own time, practicing her dancing and proverbs: the Bible and a little dance were a girl's way to salvation, if you counted a good man as salvation, which Betsey did. Talking to herself had never bothered Betsey at all. Why Tina Turner even said, "There Is Something on My Mind," and there was always something on Betsey's mind.

Etta James crooned something low and nasty in the background. Betsey's little backside went everywhichaway trying to keep in the correct ambiance. "What am I 'sposed to do? Be deaf, dumb, and blind? A girl's gotta practice her dancin, the fast as well as the slow kind. Be up on her Bible and the ways of the Negroes from Akron Ohio all the way to Machito. I'm gettin too big to play tie-em up and skidaddle with Dale and Joe. I'm more of a heifer now than they'll ever know."

Betsey laughed out loud, remembering being the calf the ropers were to brand by mixing spit and dirt on their hands and rubbing it on the cheek of the heifer. Pretty soon, as they got older, the cheek wasn't anywhere near her lips, but closer to her thighs. Her mama liked a died, seein that husky Dale and the tallest Joe this side of Enright Street rubbing Betsey's behind. No, she was way too big for games like that now. She had to practice her steps, the way Mama and Daddy did when they went out dancing, or to a formal or a masquerade ball. She'd have to know which hand to hold out and which foot to move 'fore the next, when to turn, if the pull to the left meant turn right or turn left or just stop till the next measure. A girl had to practice her dancing, which is exactly what Betsey Brown was in the process of doing when Jane's voice plummeted down the stairs once again.

"Betsey, I thought I told you to turn that mess off!"

As Jane's reprimand sailed down the stairs, it muffled the little feet of Sharon and Margot eager to tease Betsey and still getta chance to hear a little blues.

"Didn't you hear Mama say to turn that mess off," Margot whispered, turning herself to the arm of Greer's favorite chair.

"Yeah, didn't you hear Mama say to cut that mess off," Sharon giggled, doing the bop the wrong way.

"I have my reasons," Betsey said and kept on with the intricacies of everything she could imagine a colored boy trying to have her do on a dance floor without ever once opening his mouth, which would mean she was a good dancer cause you don't have to talk to a good dancer, they just feel what the next step is and do it. That's what Betsey had on her mind and her body sashayed and flung itself cross the carpet over to the speaker, past Sharon's off-time little numbers, round Margot's awkward turns and turn again..

"Girl, you a niggah to your very soul." Margot stopped, out of breath and envious. "I can't imagine what a child like you is even doing in this house."

Sharon grabbed Margot's hand and said something Betsey couldn't hear, but surely had to do with stealing from Vida's cookie jar and messing with Betsey's mind. They ran off to the pantry together mimicking Jane. "Turn that mess off, Betsey. Betsey that niggah noise is disturbing my rest."

Betsey stopped dead in her tracks. She'd had enough of all of this. Every time she played music she was a niggah. If she mentioned Nasser, she was a communist. If she wanted to boycott her school, she was a rabble-rouser. If she wanted to eat at Howard Johnson's, she was giving whites more than was their due. No matter what she said or did, it wasn't right. In addition to the fact that she hadn't been kissed since Eugene Boyd came calling that first evening. It was plain as could be to anyone with good sense, with the head God put on her shoulders, that the only reasonable thing to do was run away. That was clear as day.

Betsey turned the music way down low and let the rhythm help her figure her future. Her life wasn't going to be another Nadinaola meets Duke Pomade affair. She was gonna be in the trenches for the race, she'd win the dance trophies, put the white folks in their place. She'd paint her nails and wax her bangs, she'd do everything the bad girls did. Oh, she was gonna run away and see what the truth of the matter was.

Now, what should she call herself for this great journey? Sojourner she was not. The lady was still too much alive.

Susan B. Anthony was a white woman. But Cora, Cora was a calling name. Cora Sue Betsey Anne with a "e" Calhoun (to make sure they'd know she was colored) Brown. Cora Sue Betsey Anne Calhoun Brown.

"I'ma big girl now with ideas of my own. These crazy folks round here just won't leave me alone. 'Turn that mess off, Betsey.' 'Betsey you know you're tryin your best to be a niggah.' As if I had anything to do with that. That was God's will is what it was. How can you try to be what you awready are? Sometimes these folks just don't make no sense at all. 'Betsey, you could do better than to let the whole world know you a niggah.'

"These crazy people just won't leave me alone and this is my mama I'm talking bout, my daddy, my home. I've gotta find some place to be on my own, where I don't have to explain and where I'm never ashamed that I'm Miss Cora Sue Betsey Anne Calhoun Brown."

For some reason hearin Chuck Jackson singing made Betsey wanta get married. This is, after she'd run away and made a career of her own, like her mama had and Madame C. J. Walker. Oh yes, Betsey Calhoun would be coming to the altar with something of her own to offer, but who was to be the groom?

When I get married I could be Mrs. Cora Sue Betsey Anne Calhoun Eisenhower. I could marry the President, or maybe even Duke Ellington. That would make me a Duchess. Duchess Cora Sue Betsey Anne Calhoun Ellington. If one of them died I could marry Bobby Jackson from the eighth grade, but he's so colored, even I recognize that. No, I'ma stick with Eisenhower or Ellington. Oh, but what about "Sugar" Ray

Robinson? He's so handsome. He's so sharp. Mrs. Cora Sue Betsey Anne Calhoun Brown "Sugar" Robinson. Sounds good to me. I'd still have to have my own career, maybe a philosopher or an actress like Dandridge or Eartha. An intellectual like Mama should have married W.E.B. DuBois. I wonder why Mama didn't marry ol' W.E.B.? He wasn't half so dark as Daddy and to my knowledge he didn't play the drums every morning, either. But there's no telling what can get on a person's mind when they're in love. Mama must just love Daddy to death the way she be screaming at him sometimes. But I like my daddy too, I just can't marry him cause then what would Mama do? When I marry the President I shall call Eugene to be my escort cause "Ike" will have to go visit some troops about the colored and I'll have a big party for all the colored who live in Little Rock, Arkansas, with barbeque and cannons and lotsa root beer, just for the colored.

I'm Miss Cora Sue Betsey Anne Calhoun Brown, soon to be married to a Negro man of renown. There's Cab Calloway. Machito. Mongo Santamaria. Tito Puente. Colonel Davis. Nasser. Nkrumah. James Brown. No, that won't do, cause I'd be Mrs. Brown-Brown. And what about Eugene Boyd? I'll elope, that's what. Marry him first and then I'll tell him about the President and all.

"Betsey, I thought I told you to turn off that mess!" Jane meant business this time.

"Daughter, there's no need to raise your voice this time of night," Vida sighed from the parlor.

"Betsey's still downstairs, Mama. I saw her," Sharon cried out.

"There's no need to tell on people just to be telling on

them," Greer responded matter-of-factly to Sharon's brilliant espionage.

Jane slithered underneath her husband's torso. "Nobody had to tell me anything. You've got Betsey thinking she's the queen of the blues, but I got news for you, buddy."

Greer fell asleep to dreams of perfect sutures and Jane rubbed her left eye once more. Her left eye always jumped when something was amiss. A mess. Her life was a mess. Her left eye was jumping. "Give me a hot dog and a barrel of beer" kept running through her brain. Betsey musta gone to bed. That hellish music was off downstairs. Yet Bessie Smith was going on in her head. She wisht her eye would stop jumping like that. What could possibly be the matter? There wasn't a soul stirring in the Brown house. Quiet as it could be. Too quiet. Why'd he fall asleep. Damn hospital. "The joint is jumping, it's really jumping" rambled through Jane's sleep.

Besides Betsey there was no one about except Vida, who was singing on Jesus in her bedroom. "Jesus Is My Beloved" Vida sang as Betsey was moving her bags down the back stairs to the side porch so she could make off to Mrs. Maureen's insteada going to that simple-ass school one more day. She had everything she needed. Late in the night with the flashlight reserved for tornadoes and blizzards, Betsey had picked *The Best of Nat King Cole*, *Etta Sings For You*, Tina Turner in the multiples and Jackie Wilson's "Doggin Me Around." There was Toussaint l'Ouverture's biography, a picture of Langston Hughes, a drawing of Billie Holiday, a tennis ball that Althea Gibson had hit on, a copy of the Negro National Anthem, and a few clothes. She prayed her father wouldn't notice, but she'd made off with one of Dizzy Gillespie's mouthpieces, too. That was in case she needed to sell something to have some money. She'd heard that song bout "getting a job" ringing in her head: "And when I get the papers, I read em thru and thru, to find out if there is any work for me."

Betsey was very organized bout the whole thing. She was going to go over to Mrs. Maureen's where the ladies came to get their heads done. She would learn a decent trade, not have to be worried bout white folks cause there weren't none around there, hear all bout the Shirelles and Dinah Washington, Mrs. Briscoe and Sister Auroralia who could see into the future for a price. This was gonna be Betsey Brown's new life.

Betsey went out the back door, saw the half moon and smelled the damp night. She planned to go through the back yards of all the houses before Union Boulevard. Then she would take the bus round to Kingshighway, walk up it, and rest on Wabada Street. That would be half the journey to Mrs. Maureen's. The moon was now skirted with thick clouds. Betsey started to hurry off, but realized she didn't have to do anything unless she felt like it. Wouldn't Mrs. Maureen be surprised to see her!

There was nothing like the smell of five or six newly pressed heads mingling with different types of greases and oils, long with the chicken brought in from next door or the ribs from cross the street. The jukebox justa goin cause women liked to be sung to while they were prettying themselves up. That's how Mrs. Maureen put it. The curling irons would be clacking, bringing that last little old piece of hair up under the iron, so a row of curls enveloped the thinnest or broadest of faces. A row of curls a minute long or a row of curls flowing down your back. That's how good Mrs. Maureen was at her trade. She took em with good hair, bleached or colored hair, hardly no hair to good-as-white-folks' hair. Made no difference to her. If you paid your bill and walked out with a smile, Mrs. Maureen was satisfied.

Now "satisfaction" was something that Mrs. Maureen always discussed with Betsey. "Satisfaction" was the calling card of a good man, the Lord, and a night on the town. Yes sirree, to be "satisfied" was to know no wants or cravings and, hallelujah, never be in a envious state of mind. Be satisfied. Get what you want. Get somebody to get it for you, but have that sense in your soul, in your bones that "na'chel" knowledge of what is satisfaction. Mrs. Maureen told Betsey this cause so many of her clients, that's the women whose heads she did, were not satisfied and so complained about every little doggone thing, got to looking old too soon and trying to pull hips too big for a growed elephant up the stairs to Maureen's House of Beauty on Easton Boulevard. Yes, Mrs. Maureen would be clicking those curling irons or running that hot comb right next to your scalp talking bout the necessities of satisfaction in a woman's life. Said she could see a unsatisfied woman with her head turned backwards and the lights out. There was a certain smell to a woman what knows satisfaction.

Mrs. Maureen knew more bout women and they needs than anyone sides Jesus, far as Betsey could tell. Why once when Betsey was under the dryer, which Mrs. Maureen liked her to be more often than not, Betsey heard the whole room of ladies laughing cause one Reverend's wife had been calling on Jesus to "fix her." Betsey heard Mrs. Maureen say she couldn't have no heavenly mechanic working with her parts. Betsey wasn't 'sposed to have heard that. But she already knew the song,

"Fix Me, Jesus, Fix Me." Vida sang it in the evenings sometimes or when she was crying bout Frank being gone. A mechanic could do "it" or Heavenly Son Jesus could do "it." There was that "it" again. Some "it" a woman's gotta have satisfied or be in trouble. Mrs. Maureen also believed wholeheartedly that unsatisfied women were mean and just a mess of trouble. That's how come she told Betsey to find her a man what could satisfy her every need. Then Betsey said that only the Lord Almighty was able to do that. Mrs. Maureen just chuckled down in her full brown belly.

"The Lord done put a heap of glory in the bodies of many a young man, cause He just be overwhelmed with satisfying so many souls. The Lord needed some working man's he'p sometime, that all." And Betsey's head was done.

Now these curls would have to stay in they tight little rows till one of Mrs. Maureen's helpers gave you a comb-out, otherwise known as a style. But Mrs. Brown liked those curls to set right on her girls' heads cause she didn't trust Mrs. Maureen's assistants not to send her children home looking too grown or colored.

Now, Mrs. Maureen had always been honest with Betsey and let her know from the start that God had not given her the best head of hair in the world, but it was workable and had a chestnut sheen to it that made it stand out from everybody else's. Yep, it wasn't the thickest or longest head of hair, but good strong nappy hair. That it was. There was something to it that reminded Mrs. Maureen of the way hair grew on heads in Mississippi where her folks lived and that's why Mrs. Maureen felt a special feeling for Betsey, being almost like home folks as she was. That's why Betsey thought the most reasonable place to go when she ran away was to Mrs. Maureen's, where she could learn more bout satisfaction and earn a decent day's pay by sweeping all the cut hair up off the floor, fetching dinners and sodas for the ladies, bringing them *Ebony*, *Sepia*, or *Jet*, holding the mirrors so they could see how they hair was really set. Yes, Mrs. Maureen's for some Snickers and a few Red Hots from behind the container of hairpins at the last booth where Mrs. Maureen always acted so surprised to have found them.

Betsey had taken so many out of the way turns she almost got lost. Plus she was a little sleepy and tired from carrying her bags. The moon was completely effaced by dark clouds on a dark night. Betsey headed straightaway for Mrs. Maureen's, but fell asleep under someone's porch.

When Betsey woke, she used dewy leaves to clean her face and pushed her hair around till it felt neat. She brushed off her skirt and was on her way.

It wasn't like she was going to Paris or anything like Josephine Baker, but Betsey did have a feeling of adventure about her when she boarded the trolley with her small suitcase and her candies. It was nice to be on the trolley heading toward the colored section of town for a change. She wouldn't be seeing no white folks today. That was one thing for sure. Just some police, maybe. That's all. She wouldn't be seeing too much of anybody, actually. Everybody was going in the other direction. Weren't many jobs round Mrs. Maureen's way and folks what had em lived there anyhow, so they didn't have to take no trolley.

EIGHT

Not too much was happening round Mrs. Maureen's at that early hour of the morning. Mr. Tavaneer was winding the gates up in fronta his liquor store. The grease wasn't even hot yet in Mrs. Jackson's "We Know You Like Jackson's Chicken House." Mrs. Maureen didn't have her blinking lights on either. Mrs. Maureen's blinking lights were a silhouette of a bouffant hairdo with the words "Maureen Can Do This For You" underneath in blue and red. The hairdo was purple and didn't blink. Some of the lights were out, but everybody knew where Mrs. Maureen's was. Betsey had to shout "Hello" to

Mr. Tavaneer cause one time some robbers shot a pistol right upside his head for not moving fast enough. Mr. Tavaneer said he never had no intentions of moving, but no one knew the rest of the story cause the robbers hightailed it on away. Just Mr. Tavaneer couldn't hear.

"Hello, Mr. Tavaneer!" Betsey walked closer to him. "Good Morning, Mr. Tavaneer!" Betsey was almost shouting by now. Mr. Tavaneer turned round gruffly. "Must you be blasting the daylights out of the ground, Betsey? It's the other side I can't hear out of, not this one. What you doing round here so early in the morning? Mrs. Maureen aint open to customers at this hour."

"Oh, I'm not coming as a customer, Mr. Tavaneer. I'm looking for work."

Betsey set her things down as Mr. Tavaneer opened the Spirit Shop.

"Aint your father still a doctor?"

"Yes, Sir."

"Don't your mama work round to the hospital with them crazy folks?"

"Yes, Sir."

"Then why do you need work?"

"That's how come I came to see Mrs. Maureen."

"At this hour?" Mr. Tavaneer swept the debris from in front of his store and stepped back, surveying the neighborhood. The crap games would start soon. The laundrymats'd be open. The numbers man would be coming by a few times. The winos would find their way to his shop and the smell would lift him nigh unto heaven's gate.

"Well, you keep a good ten feet from either side of my

store, Betsey. That's all I need is for the police to say I been catering to minors. Sides, I gotta mind to call your papa. I know he don't think you out this way looking for no job. I just might do that. Silly gal. You'll find out soon enough St. Louis is a dangerous place."

Betsey wasn't thrilled with Mr. Tavaneer's words for the day, but she went on up the stairs to Mrs. Maureen's anyway. At first there was no answer. Betsey rang the bell again and still nobody came.

"I told you it was a peculiar hour to come round Mrs. Maureen's to 'work.'" Mr. Tavaneer shouted from his bad side, thinking Betsey couldn't hear him.

By the third ring, Betsey was beginning to feel a little scared. It was awfully quiet and dingy. There were ill-meaning folks cluttering up the street. Mrs. Maureen's looked worn-out, or needing something like the Saturday customers to spruce it up. Finally Mrs. Maureen came down the many steps to the door. Her face wasn't as pleasant as usual. That's cause all the make-up from the night before hadn't been properly oiled away yet. Then, too, Mrs. Maureen didn't have on her beauty salon uniform. She had on a robe of some sort that twisted round her body like the ripples in some kinds of soda bottles, round and round, till they reached her bosom where they stopped all of a sudden and all this flesh hung out in two great mounds, dusted with little red feathers.

"Betsey Brown, is that you?" Mrs. Maureen managed to whisper through a wig that was sitting on her head the wrong way, or at least lopsided. "Well, Betsey, I aint open now. I mean, aint it a bit early to come callin?"

"Yes, Mrs. Maureen. I'm very sorry to disturb you, but I

didn't know where else to go. I ran away and you're the only person I know who might help me."

Mrs. Maureen put her hand on her hip to help herself stand up.

"You say you ran away. You ran away from where?"

"From home, Mrs. Maureen. I ran away from home. Nobody understands me there. They all want me to be somebody else. And I'm just Betsey Brown, Mrs. Maureen. You understand, don't you?"

Mrs. Maureen's eyes were finally beginning to come open. She coughed to wake up and shifted the tottering wig to the other side of her head.

"Un, hum. You say you ran away and came here." It took a long time for Mrs. Maureen to grasp the reality of Betsey's announcement. Now Mrs. Maureen had all kinds of girls coming in and out, but they weren't thirteen, or plain old "Betsey Browns." "Yes, you come on in heah while I think on this some. Run away, hum? And you ran away over heah?"

"Yes, M'am."

Mrs. Maureen's eyes kept opening and shutting as she led Betsey up the stairs to the beauty parlor, or what Betsey knew of the beauty parlor. Behind the French doors where Betsey assumed Mrs. Maureen lived, there was indeed a kitchen, but there were also some roomers or callers or men and women in the midst of all sorts of transactions. Betsey most forgot where she was and was fixing to run home till she remembered she was running away from home.

Mrs. Maureen shooed everyone out her way. Made herself a pot of coffee.

"You eat?"

"Yes, M'am." Betsey was having second thoughts about coming to Mrs. Maureen's. Seemed like there was more going on than usual. There were never any men at Mrs. Maureen's, and the girls who helped out wore uniforms from the uniform store like Mrs. Maureen's. It didn't smell old and tired. Mrs. Maureen never looked so old, either.

Once she had her coffee and her body stopped this persistent heaving and swaying with every sigh, Mrs. Maureen took Betsey's hands up in hers and said, "Chile, I know folks that love you can't always see exactly what you mean, or feel exactly how you feel, but I can't let you stay here in a place like this. Why I wouldn't even let one of my own daughters stay here, Betsey."

"But, Mrs. Maureen, you said I was almost like kinfolk. You said there was folks in Mississippi who looked like me. You said you'd love to have a child like me around to chat with and grow up."

"Oh, Betsey, chile, I know your mama's missing you."

Mrs. Maureen kept rubbing her hands together with Betsey's, as if rubbing hands together would rub the knowledge of the world into Betsey's head.

"But Mrs. Maureen, please, please don't call Mama. She doesn't even know I'm gone yet. They think I'm at school."

"And that's where you should be."

"I'm tired of those white folks."

"Who you think aint tired of white folks?"

Mrs. Maureen was beginning to get mad at Betsey now. Of all the very last nerve, to be running away from a family as nice as the Browns. Betsey needed a good talking to.

"Well, now that you've run off and all, what are you gointa

do?" Mrs. Maureen shoved a plate of grits and eggs and sausage under Betsey's chin, while she waited for a response.

"I was gonna help you out in the shop until I eloped."

Mrs. Maureen liked to fell off her chair which would have been quite something, seeing how Mrs. Maureen was quite something.

"Elope?"

"Yes, M'am." Betsey's eyes gleamed as she said the word and tasted the peppers in the sausage.

Mrs. Maureen, who knew she was getting on in years and had heard just about everything there was to hear and seen more than there was to see, let herself light up the kitchen with laughter. "Elope." Mrs. Maureen jumped up like she was twirling crepe paper for a wedding screaming: "Elope," and trailing it with, "Where you goin'? To Arkansas? Chirren can't get married in Missouri and believe me, I know about the law. And that's the law."

When she'd tired herself out, Mrs. Maureen asked Betsey: "Isn't elopin a bit ol' fashioned? How old is this boy and does he know too, or is this thing just a secret tween me and you?"

Betsey didn't see anything funny about her situation. She especially didn't think her friend, Mrs. Maureen, should be laughing at her this way. Eugene Boyd was a fine boy and thirteen was just a little way from being full grown. But it was Mrs. Maureen's or she didn't know what, so Betsey kept her mouth shut.

"Hum, elope? Hum. I've heard that one before. Sorry to say."

Mrs. Maureen started to clear the dishes away. The morning

throng began to mill about once again in tee-shirts and robes, nighties and nothing.

"If you're gonna stay with us, you might as well see it in the raw, honey." Mrs. Maureen rubbed Betsey's back, which was stiff as a rail. "Don't worry, nobody's gonna hurt you."

Betsey wisht she was home. Right now. Away from these men with stocking caps on and curlers in their heads. These women with too much rouge and not enough clothes.

"Betsey, I think a friend of yours ran away to me some time ago. I think she's still here. Let me go see. She was gointa elope, too, I recollect. Folks round your way sho' don't be keepin up with the times. Elope. Two colored chirren elopin. I swear I hear all the bad news first. Even 'fore the President, they let me in on it. REGINA! Regina, bring your hot lil tail out here and talk some sense to this gal bout love and romance. Regina!"

Betsey watched as women passed by the kitchen table leaving wads of money in the center. The men with rollers strolled by too, pulling folds of dollar bills from their money clips. There was a lot of money on that table. More money than when she and Margot and Sharon emptied Greer's pockets and Jane's purses in order to go to the movies that time Jane and Greer went to Paris and left them with some skinny woman whose baby stank. There was really a lot of money on that table by the time Mrs. Maureen appeared with Regina. It hadn't occurred to Betsey that Regina could be Roscoe's Regina from love and kisses, but there she was in a awful flimsy red negligee, deep holes under her eyes, and a shame on her that made Betsey's skin cringe. Regina was pregnant. She laid her money on Mrs. Maureen's table too.

"Now do like I tol' you and tell this girl bout runnin off and elopin and carryin on like a fool over some no count niggah with his head fulla dreams. Go on, do like I say."

Regina and Betsey hugged and hugged. Regina's tummy bumping Betsey's head. Betsey thought she could hear the baby singing. She knew she could hear it moving. Regina's stomach was so hard, like a drum. Betsey knew from the tears in Regina's eyes that the baby was Roscoe's.

"Gina, where's Roscoe? I thought youall were going to Chicago to have your family?"

"Guess who's in Chi-town, Betsey?" Mrs. Maureen asked, counting her money.

"Roscoe's getting things ready for us, Betsey. Honest he is. He told me to stay here till he could send for me. Said it wouldn't take long."

"And how many weeks you been here now? You'll still be here when that baby comes flying outta ya."

"He told me I was coming here to work for you."

"He didn't tell me you couldn't press heads, so I put you to work doing what you obviously knew how to do awready."

Betsey helped Regina sit down. Gina couldn't stop crying or holding her tummy, her baby. She kept whispering Roscoe's name, praying for him to come get her. She was bout to lose her mind. Betsey held onto her real tight. She remembered Roscoe standing up to Grandma. She was sure Roscoe loved Regina. She was sure Roscoe didn't know the kinda trouble Regina was in.

"Regina, I know Roscoe loves you. I was there. I saw you kiss. He's gonna send for you. Believe me." Betsey pulled closer to Regina's naked legs, swollen and overperfumed.

"You think so, Betsey? You think he's gonna get me outta heah?"

"You can get outta heah anytime you pay me the money you owe me for your room and board."

"Mrs. Maureen, I could stay and help you press heads. Mommy lets me press Margot and Sharon's sometimes when they need a touch-up. I'll help Regina and that way I could stay with you, too. Would that be awright with you, Gina?"

"Oh, Betsey, you can't stay here. There's too much going on that I don't want you to see, ever. Things I never want you or my baby to see."

"Looks to me like you saw a bit too much 'fore you came prancin through my front door, missie. Don't you be holdin me responsible for your behavior."

Mrs. Maureen divided the money in small stacks, which were picked up by the strangely clad women who'd put it there. The largest portion went right in the cleft of Mrs. Maureen's bosom. She patted it over and over, smiling at Betsey. She did like Betsey.

"Girl, why don't we go in the other room and I'll do your head up real pretty, with some bumper curls we'll comb out together. You got to go home, chile. I know your mama's missing you. A sweet chile like you got no business here 'cept on Saturday mornings when your head needs doing. C'mon, let's get the combs heated up."

"No, Mrs. Maureen. Let me stay at least long enough to help with Regina's baby. I could baby-sit, you know that, and help you keep the place straight." Betsey was frightened. How could Roscoe leave Regina like this? What was Gina doing with all that money and the baby? How could being in love leave you so sad and alone? "Mrs. Maureen, please let me stay, just a few days? Mama won't be mad when she knows I've been with you."

"Your mama aint never gointa know you been with me. Her heart's probably breaking right this minute, wondering where is that bright sweet girl she loves so much. And here you are making a fuss over a fool gal got herself knocked-up and left behind."

Mrs. Maureen was fiddling with Betsey's braids now. Taking them down one by one and running her fingers through the hair looking for split ends she'd have to cut.

"You think that school won't call your mama and tell her you aint there? What you think she's gonna imagine? Well, let me tell you. She's gointa think some crackers got hold to you and beat you good! That's what! This city is going to the dogs these days. I'm tellin you. Gina, go on and tell her what I tol' you. Do like I say, now."

Regina's eyes were sunken and swollen now. She knew Betsey couldn't stay at Mrs. Maureen's. That was out of the question, but she didn't want Betsey to think that love left you pitiful like that song went, "They Call Me, Mr. Pitiful." Gina wanted Betsey to remember the joy and the hope of two hands joined, swinging down the street. She also wanted Betsey to have hope for her.

"Listen, I've got an idea. Mrs. Maureen, why don't you do Betsey's hair, while I give her a manicure."

"Least you learned to do that."

"No, now let me finish. I'll give Betsey a manicure and a pedicure. Then we could do her face up like in the Ebony Fashion Fair. That way, when she does get home, she'll be looking so pretty her mama will forget how mad she is. You know she's going to be mad, don't you, Betsey?"

"Yeah, but it's her fault. She won't let me play the music I want to hear or dance the way I want to dance. You know, Regina, how we usedta fool around at Soldan when Smokey Robinson came, or the time you took us to see the Olympics. We danced in the aisles with everybody else. It was so wonderful when you were there, Regina. Remember, we did routines from the Shirelles and you rolled our hair up like the Ronettes with those false hairpieces from Mr. Robinson's. She doesn't want me to be like everybody else, Regina. She wants me to be special, like I lived inside a glass cage or something. She actually thinks those white kids where I go to school think I'm alive. Gina, they hardly speak to me. And the one time I had a spend-the-night party only one of them showed up, and she was Jewish. They don't like her, either. But I can't tell anybody these things cause how would that look, to say we weren't up to white folks. I know we got to fight the white people and be better than them, Gina. It's just I'm so tired of them and I feel so much better when I'm with the colored. I feel so much better when I'm like everybody else."

Betsey wept on Gina's thighs just where the baby was jutting out. Mrs. Maureen was mixing egg yolks and beer to give Betsey a conditioner, shaking her head, mumbling bout the things children had on their minds these days. A child had a right to be a child. Even in Mississippi a girl was a girl till her time came. White folks or no white folks. Nobody sent a little ol' thing out to take up for the whole damn race. That's what was wrong with the colored, always putting it off to the next generation to do battle with the white man.

"Betsey, honey, that's called loneliness. You're gonna be lonely sometimes, sweetie. Cause you are special. Your mama's not making that up. You are different and it's not the color of your skin, either. You have a good time the way nobody else can, and you feel things the way nobody else can. There is no such thing as ordinary, Betsey. Nobody's ordinary. Each one of us is special and it's the coming together of alla that that makes the world so fine."

Mrs. Maureen almost dropped her egg yolks and beer concoction, listening to Gina. Then she motioned for Gina to move Betsey's head round so they could condition it real good.

"Betsey, I'm not saying that there's not different kinds of folks. You and me, we're different."

"You better believe that," Mrs. Maureen added, her fingers gooey with the yolk and malt coating Betsey's head.

"That's not what I meant, but in a way it is. Betsey, you and I can do certain kinds of things together and then there are other things we can never do together. It's hard to explain, but there's all different kinds of colored folks. You're one kind and I'm another, that's all."

"But don't you like me, Regina?"

"Oh Betsey, I love you. You're like my own sister. Why if the baby is a girl, I'ma gonna name her Elizabeth and call her Betsey with a 'e.' Cross my heart."

"She's ready for a rinse now." Mrs. Maureen wrapped Betsey's head in a towel, while Regina threw an old shirt around Betsey's very Lord and Taylor school outfit.

Regina laughed silently. Betsey even ran off like a doctor's daughter. How was she going to be ordinary when there weren't but five thousand Negro doctors in the whole country. Gina'd heard Dr. Brown say that to Charlie one time, when Charlie said he wanted to be like Jackie Robinson. What a whipping that was. Thinking bout the Browns took Regina's mind off Betsey and to her baby.

How was she gonna feed her child? How could she ever have a child like Betsey, who heard the word colored and thought of something good? How was she gonna explain who or where Daddy was, when she'd planned for Daddy to be right there?

The rinse was set and Betsey was under the dryer in the front of Mrs. Maureen's, where the hincty Negro ladies lined up with their furs and polished faces. Mrs. Maureen's demeanor had changed entirely, as had her clothes. She was in her little pink uniform with the appliquéd flower on the collar and the white nurse's shoes she wore every day as she stood over the doctor's wife, the lawyer's wife, the minister's wife, and the undertaker's wife. The helpers were clad in smart white jackets moving quickly from hand to hand, foot to foot. It was the only place in town a Negro woman could get a manicure or a pedicure, if she was brave enough. They lived in a world of their own and never ventured past the French doors where Mrs. Maureen's other world thrived.

Betsey was as pampered as a princess. Mrs. Maureen explained her presence on a school day as a mixture of a birthday present and as a prelude to Betsey's solo clarinet performance in front of the white people at one of those "schools."

The women nodded their heads. Yes, it was important to look good if you're dealing with white folks. Yes, it was lovely of Mrs. Brown to think of letting Betsey have a manicure when her hands were going to be so prominently displayed.

Betsey couldn't hear, but she could see some of what Regina meant. There were different kinds of Negroes. She bet money some of these Negroes wouldn't give a stone's throw if something happened to Roscoe, they didn't care what was gonna happen to Regina's baby. "Niggahs" they'd say and leave it to the will of God that people, especially colored people, suffered. Yet, they couldn't go anywhere else to have their hands done but a bordello. Betsey burst out laughing. She could tell by the looks on the women's faces that it was an "inappropriate" laugh. As if being a Negro was appropriate. Betsey knew they'd never get that joke. So she went back to reading bout a murder in *Tan*.

Mrs. Maureen sent Regina for Little John to come do Betsey's make-up. It was Mrs. Maureen's way of saying to Mrs. Brown that there's a growing girl here, lady, pay attention. The minister's wife left just in time. The other ladies were puzzled, but calmed when Mrs. Maureen went on bout stagelights and bone structure. Little John just hovered with brushes of mink and fox hair. He was in his world. A face with no wrinkles. No blemishes. Purity. He was beside himself. Mrs. Maureen had to remind him, "Little John, she a child playing a clarinet, this is not the Jewel Box Revue."

The pedicure Regina executed herself. She wanted Betsey to feel relaxed and cared about. The way all little Negro girls should feel. Not cramped or out of place, or funny-looking or easy. Just lovely and well-loved. Gina gave Betsey a very special pedicure cause she knew she'd never have one, and probably her little girl wouldn't either. Not the way this world was bout folks born on the other side of the tracks, colored or white. You could forget it, the sweetness, that is.

Betsey could hardly believe it was her when she looked in the mirror. What a woman she was going to be! Regina gave her five dollars to take a cab home, cause dusk was falling and it was getting late. Regina made her promise not to come back or mention to her mama about the baby or Roscoe. Mrs. Maureen was more explicit.

"If your mother so much as dreams you were here before the shop opened, you gonna get a licking the likes of which you've never felt."

Regina held Betsey real close to her. "Betsey, your life isn't gonna be like mine. Don't you grow up too soon. Take your time. There's something so special when you're really in love, let it come to you. Don't chase it. Okay? You be good, now. I love you."

With that Betsey was sent down the stairs and out the door, escorted by Little John, who was still dabbing and brushing her face. "You are just too beautiful, my dear."

Betsey felt beautiful. She felt brave. She knew it now. There was a difference between being a little girl and being a woman. She knew now. She'd never see Regina again, but they'd never be separate, either. Women who can see over the other side are never far from each other.

Betsey took her five dollars to a very special place. A Yellow cab carried her to the boulevard where the white folks had their parade each fall and crowned a queen of the Veiled Prophet, who was a white man no one ever saw. Then they had a big ball with pictures in the newspapers for days of this white girl and that white girl. The regular people could come and watch, even the colored. Betsey did it every year, looked at the floats of the ladies in waiting in their satin gowns and laced gloves, the clowns and musicians longside the floats entertaining one and all. The whole city in a Mardi Gras out of season and out of time, with young girls of every color wishing the man behind the jeweled mask had chosen them to ride about the city that night, a night the stars were sapphires, opals, and diamonds, a tiara for a queen.

Betsey paid the cab driver $4.25 and gave him the rest as a tip. She was feeling regal. Then she marched as grandly as possible to the middle of the street where she proceeded to stop traffic and create a great stir while she declared herself Queen of the Negro Veiled Prophet and his entourage.

The police only asked her her name and address, and went on about how St. Louis was a dangerous place to be roaming about alone at dusk. They didn't understand she reigned on her own streets for the first time in her life. She wasn't afraid anymore. The city was hers.

NINE

Jane's chandeliers were the hallmark of her move south. She had no winding staircase with mahogany rail, but she had chandeliers of every shape and size. The chandelier in the dining room hung down like a soft skirt, rows of crystal looping back to the center where the candlelight bulbs left a sheen of rose over the good table. In the first living room the chandelier etched a diamond shape, glistening tinkles reflecting the rise of the race, the status of the bridge players. The third chandelier was one large circle of hexagonal crystals coming to a point directly above Jane's head where she knelt in the midst of all her family praying for her daughter's safe return.

"Jesus, please let us have our girl back. My child knows we love her. We don't know what brought her to leave us, but Lord, Jesus Christ, please keep her safe until the very moment she walks back through that door. And we know she'll be coming back to us, Lord, because You are a Benevolent Savior, a Gentle Redeemer, and a gracious host of all living creatures. This we pray, Dear Lord, please bring our Betsey back."

Jane knelt silently with tears rolling down her cheeks. Sharon and Margot were afraid. They were praying, but not knowing the faith Jane and Vida knew, they feared the loss of their big sister to some evil in the city, a maniac. She might disappear like the children they heard about on the radio sometimes who went to school and never came back. Children who weren't even planning to run away. Allard whimpered every once in a while, "I want Betsey now, Mama." Then Vida would hum "Pass Me Not, Oh Gentle Savior" and rock him till he quieted. Charlie was uneasy in this room saturated with pleas to Christ, but he knew enough that Betsey needed some power besides her own wherever in the hell she'd carried herself off to. Once the room was calm, Jane would begin to pray aloud again.

"Dear Lord, we don't know where our child is, but we know You do. Because You know all things and all the ways of this world. In Thy sight somewhere our child is wrestling with wrongdoing, Lord. Come to her aid and bring her back to us. She shall be received as was the Prodigal Son. We shall open our hearts to her, Lord, we promise to make her home a place she'll never want to leave again. But, first, Lord, please bring Betsey back to us, sound of body and sound of mind."

Greer had called the police hours before and sat in the

kitchen by the phone tying surgical knots to the ends of his conga drum, pursing his lips. Greer was a warm man, but not a churchgoing man. He was more worried about the police not giving a damn about a missing colored child than he was that Betsey would be mangled by some deranged stranger. Greer had faith in his people, not in Jesus, not in the police, not in the pastor called to comfort Vida, already mildly sedated to prevent aggravation of her heart.

Not being a man of God did not make him a distant man. His hands fumbled one of the knots and the veins in his temples jumped, thinking what would become of his daughter in a city that might as well be below the Mason-Dixon Line, where plenty of colored made their way on the wrong side of everything. Now Betsey was out there with them. Greer knew she'd gone to one of the Negro neighborhoods, but he couldn't set his mind on which one. All the note said was:

> I love you all very much, but I
> don't belong here. I'm different
> from you all. Take good care of
> Margot and Sharon. Charlie be a
> doctor. Please watch Allard and
> those fires. Tell Eugene he'll have to
> look for me when I'm grown-up. I
> love you,
>
> Betsey

Greer had gone over the note again and again, trying to imagine what made Betsey think she didn't belong at home, that she couldn't grow at home, that her house wasn't as full of good colored as the next. He tried to tie more surgical knots, but as the tension and anger grew in him, his fingers began to beat a bomba on the conga drum.

Jane leapt to her feet, virtually flying into the kitchen.

"You goddamned black niggah! Can't you understand my child's missing and you have the nerve to be in here playing those stupid drums. African! Don't you have any sense at all? Are you out of your mind? You better get down on your knees and pray the good Lord doesn't strike you down. Heathen! Low-down colored jackass!"

Jane fell apart in Greer's arms beating his chest as he had beat the drums.

"Where's my daughter? Where's my daughter? Where's my child? Make them find her."

Greer held onto his wife. He wanted her to know he wanted Betsey back more than anything, but he couldn't kneel before a white Christ, trust the white police to do anything but ignore all his calls, the repeated inquiries, his description of his child. They all look alike. That's why Greer was always sewing up the wounds of Negroes shot "mistakenly" by the police.

He knew it was coming. He felt it when Jane pulled his hand to come to the room where the chandelier swayed from the lilt of Vida's humming and the children's building anxiety. Allard wanted to build a fire right in the middle of the room and throw precious things in it. That might bring Betsey back. Africans offered things up to the spirits and got their wishes. Indians danced and got rain. All Jane would allow was prayers to Jesus. Prayers her husband would not say. Prayers that filled his wife's very being.

Greer held back as Jane moved toward the rest of the family. Now the drumming had stopped, she was coming back to herself. She hesitated peculiarly, turned round, looked Greer straight in the eye.

"If you can't pray for your own daughter, maybe you don't belong in this house."

And off she went to the praying children, the humming Vida, and the evening lights surrounding them as though the front room was now a sanctuary.

"Dear Lord, please, see us to the safety of my child and bring her home as herself, Lord, as You know her to be and we know her."

Jane heard Greer's footsteps nearing them, she hoped he'd join them, but he turned and went up the stairs.

He'd decided to go out himself and search all the places he'd ever mentioned to Betsey, on a hunch she wanted to be an Ikette. How could he explain to Jane that Betsey wanted to be an Ikette at a time like this. Jane down there on her knees with Jesus. His whole family looked like a bad scene from *Green Pastures*.

Greer came down the stairs with great purpose and abrasiveness. Jane turned to him.

"Greer, please, I can't do this by myself. Greer, I swear if you don't join us in prayer, I'll leave you. Do you hear me? I can't do this all by myself."

Greer kept moving toward the front door.

"I thought Jesus was helping you. I'm going to find my daughter."

Jane resumed silent prayer fervently. Now she'd lost not only her daughter, but maybe her husband as well.

"Oh, where's my favorite child?" Vida murmured from the

other end of the room. The children had escaped to their individual mourning spots, asking Jesus and their private fairies to bring Betsey back. Who would they tell their secrets to? Who would have patience with Allard's shoes and his matches? Where would Charlie get girl tips from? Where was Betsey? They hadn't thought they'd miss her.

Jane helped her mother off her knees to a rocker where Vida kept asking for Betsey, which only made Jane feel more helpless now Greer was gone. But Christ was her rock, her solid ground. She went to her room to wait.

The car lurched out the driveway like a niggah gone mad, to Vida's mind. Jane dug her nails into her flesh, hoping Greer wouldn't be fool enough to drive like a jackass so some other Negro would have to sew him up tonight. Police in St. Louis didn't take kindly to Thunderbirds with out-of-state tags and a colored behind the wheel.

Vida rocked in some nether world of despair, her precious baby gone, humming "Come Thou Almighty King" intermittently, etching her hymn with verbal pleas for the safety of her grandchild.

Jane made herself a strong jigger of scotch on the rocks, sat by her vanity trying to play solitaire to pass the time, to do something with her hands, to stop crying, to keep this feeling of helplessness off her shoulder and her back. She swayed over the King and the Jack. She was blurry-eyed over the Ace and the Queen. She wanted her daughter back. She wanted her Greer back, with all his foolish ways and notions. She wanted her family to be a family again. The children were so quiet. They weren't themselves. No one was the way they usually were. All of them depending on the Grace of God and the good will of a city they still couldn't call their own.

Jane went to take a shower, steaming, then rushing cold. She washed her hair. She powdered her body till she looked like a damask mannequin. She fell asleep between two photographs: one of Betsey learning to ride a two-wheeler bike; the other of Greer in his favorite orange shirt, deep sea fishing off Atlantic City after Allard was born. She'd even done her nails. The palm of her left hand lay on top of Psalm 91:

> Whoever goes to the Lord for safety,
> whoever remains under the protection of the Almighty,
> can say to Him, "You are my defender and protector."

Greer wasn't thinking about any police. He was thinking about his daughter. Where would she go? What crazy feeling out of nowhere would come over her to take her out till all hours of the night. Maybe Jane was right. Maybe he was wrong to have filled her head with tales of Bessie Smith and Josephine Baker, let alone take her to see Jackie Wilson, Etta James, Tina Turner and the Ikettes. Maybe it wasn't right to wake up to Chico Hamilton, Lee Morgan, Charlie Parker, and Art Blakey in the morning. Watch the sunset with Miles Davis, Cecil Taylor, and Little Willie John. But Greer didn't know what else to offer that was beautiful and colored and alive, all at the same time. He drove from one club to another, thinking Betsey might be crouching by the doorway listening to some music. He thought she might be hungry so he drove past the place where Little Richard liked to get fried fish, the spot where "Sugar" Ray liked the barbeque. No Betsey. No child of his to take home.

Somewhere in the frenzy of his search for Betsey, Greer realized he'd not made rounds at the hospital. He had to make rounds. They'd write him up. He wasn't their golden boy, after all. Everybody knew he took private patients. Everybody knew he liked foreigners and was committed to causing trouble for the Negro. He had to make rounds. He went like a man at the breaking point to Homer G. Phillips Hospital to see his patients. Their lives depended on him, like his life depended on finding his Betsey.

"Why Dr. Brown, I was just going to call you. The police have Betsey in the Reception Room waiting on you. She claims to have forgotten her address and insisted that only her father would understand. Wait one second, I'll call the officers in. Patrolmen McMahon and Carlotti. Please come to Nurses Station C. Officers McMahon and Carlotti, Nurses Station C."

"Where is she, Miss Jefferson?" Greer forgot all about his patients.

"She'll be right along. The police wouldn't let her out of their sight, 'fraid she might run off again, I guess."

Greer felt a smile over his body. His hands even grinned seemed like, while he was dialing home to tell Jane Betsey was all right. Vida took the message. She said Jane was in too frail a condition to take such startling news right that minute. Vida added, "Praise Be to the Lord for this, one of His many blessings." Greer hung up the phone. His eyes filled with visions of his daughter.

"Daddy, Daddy, I knew you'd come! I knew you'd come."

Betsey leapt into her father's arms crying and smiling at once. She hugged him and kissed him, snuggled and wouldn't let go.

"Dr. Brown, I'm Officer McMahon and this is Officer Carlotti of Juvenile Affairs. Is this girl, Elizabeth Brown, your daughter?"

"Why, yes Sir. She is."

"May we see some identification, please? There are some forms you'll have to fill out. It's normal for runaways. What got me is she wouldn't say where she lived, only where you worked. We just got here before you came in. She looks to be healthy. Far as we can tell, no danger fell upon her."

Greer let Betsey down with one of those I'll-be-speaking-to-you-in-a-second looks and dealt with the officers. Betsey sat on one of the post-op tables waiting for her father. She didn't know whether to tell him all the things she'd done or be mysterious, or be plain closed-mouthed. She knew there'd be trouble at home. Boy, oh boy.

When Greer came back, he took Betsey off the table. He didn't know whether to spank her or hug her. Yet he hugged her, just the same.

"Betsey, why did you do it? Why did you run away?"

"I don't know Daddy. I had to, I guess."

"You had to run away from everybody who loves you and wants you home with them?" Greer drew his daughter under his arms and off they went on rounds, while they talked.

"Well, Daddy. I'm not like the rest of them. I mean I like music that Mommy doesn't like. I like dances Grandma swears are the Devil's doing. I like to read books way into the night and keep the other children awake. I like to make-believe there are no white people. I want my nappy hair to be pretty like Mommy's and refined like she is. And I just can't do it. So I ran away. That's all."

Greer understood some of what Betsey said. He even felt some of those things himself, sometimes, but he couldn't help laughing at one of Betsey's dilemmas. "Listen here, don't say I told you, but your mother's got a head full of nappy hair. She gets something done to it."

"Really, Daddy? Honest Injun?"

"Yep."

Greer listened to Betsey's tales of Mrs. Maureen's and, in fact, she had eaten over to the place where Little Richard ate. All the sick folks were delighted to see the doctor's little girl, but Greer was caught in the middle. Betsey'd run off for the reasons Jane'd claimed, and he had found her in that world, not even trying to go home.

Betsey and Greer said little in the car, but Greer stopped at Arnett's Fried Chicken and Shrimp joint to pick up enough food for the whole family. There was going to be some ranting and raving, but there was going to be some joy and rekindling of family spirit as well.

Betsey stole a few french fries from one of the jumbo packs, and then asked, "Is Mama real upset?"

"Yes."

"Do you think she's going to whip me?"

"I don't know."

"Did anyone miss me?"

Greer felt his heart clench at the question his daughter asked. Did anyone miss her? The whole house had been down on its knees and the wailing going on rivaled sounds heard in Jerusalem. They had a problem, a real problem, if Betsey didn't know she'd been missed, or if she felt she didn't deserve a whipping, which Greer thought he'd administer himself. The Shirelles were singing "Will you still love me tomorrow?"

Betsey thought of Eugene, who would definitely "stand by her," but she wasn't sure how her mama was going to react to all of this. Her father hadn't noticed the rouge on her cheeks, the painted nails and newly pressed head. This would be akin to a matador's cape to Jane's angry eyes when she set them on her wanton child. Betsey curled in the back seat blocking out the hollering and scolding, whipping and tustling that was coming her way. Besides, she'd had a good time, no reason to think she wouldn't have to pay for it.

Gosh, she wished her mother understood there was so much in the world to feel and see. So many things that it was just too hard to be reasonable. A girl had to get out of the house and into the thick of life, the heat of it, not knowing what all one could do with whoever you happened to be. And Betsey had just tried to be herself, where folks would assume that's how she was all the time. Herself. Plain old Betsey Brown.

Allard was the first to spy Greer and Betsey coming up the front stairs. He shouted à la Chuck Berry: "Jesus must have a telephone/ we callt on him and he brought Betsey home." Margot and Sharon joined in the chant. Vida sang a soft "Amazing Grace." Jane rushed through all of them to give her baby a hug. She held Betsey like the very flesh of her flesh had most risen from the dead. She clutched at her arms, her neck, her hair, she caressed her cheeks, her baby, safe.

"Thanks be to the Good Lord."

"She was waiting for me at the hospital," Greer bragged, pulling his wife and daughter close to him. "We're all here. Every last one of us and guess what I got?"

"Arnett's fried chicken and shrimp!" the children cried like a Greek chorus.

Vida came up to Betsey and kissed her on both cheeks,

tousled her head. "How'd you manage to get your hair done up like that, girl? I'm so glad Christ brought you back safe and sound."

Betsey hugged her grandma, little tears came to the corners of her eyes. She never intended for Vida to be in a fit. It wasn't good for her health. Vida was too near to heaven's gate for Betsey's liking anyway. What trouble she must have caused. She really could tell from the way Charlie hugged her that he'd been worried.

She'd just wanted to see the world. Marry a Negro man of renown. Change the world. Use white folks' segregated restaurant tables to dance on, and tear down all the "Colored Only" and "Colored Not Allowed" signs. She wanted to be somebody. She wanted to be Miss Elizabeth Brown out in the world, not in a house full of children still learning their tables and long division. She wanted to swing her new hairstyle and have her Humphrey Bogart not be able to keep his eyes off her, while she smuggled rifles for the Resistance. It didn't matter what movie she lived, but the woman had to be a heroine. No, a hero.

Jane swayed in Greer's arms the way she had on her wedding night. Not quite sure she was still herself, but knowing she was still in her right mind. She was so full of gratitude and love, she thought the dampness under her arms must smell of honeysuckle and dahlias, which was a very unlike Jane thought. On the other hand, Jane had never risked so much in her life: her husband and her baby. Now, just like that, the Lord had seen fit for her to know again what she sometimes forgot were blessings. A husband with ideas before their time, and a daughter with the adventure of Amelia Earhart in her soul. But they were hers. Yes, Jesus, this was her family.

"Mama, are you mad at me?" Betsey asked very quietly.

"No, I'm not mad, Betsey. I just think there are some things we have to talk about. Things we have to talk about like women together. I love you so much, darling. There's nothing you could do to change that. But don't worry now, we'll talk."

Vida had already slipped away to bed to stay on her knees a good while, thanking The Lamb of God for His Grace. The other children wandered to their rooms once all the shrimp and chicken'd disappeared.

Jane looked at Betsey's manicured hands and wondered when was the last time she'd treated herself so kindly. Years ago. It was years ago on a cruise she'd taken to Cherbourg with her new husband. Maybe Betsey's excursion wasn't just a child's first itch to be in the world. Maybe Betsey's flight offered Jane a glimpse of herself fifteen years ago, when she wasn't always shouting "no" or figuring what was for dinner. Years when she went to bed with Matisse on her mind and kisses running along her arms. Times before the children. Times Jane was not just Mommy, but a good-looking woman with a good head on her shoulders.

There wasn't much talking going on in the house that night. A calm filtered the air damp from tears and prayers. Betsey lay softly in her bed cherishing her parents' good-night kisses and remembering she was the first Negro Veiled Prophet's Queen. Jane and Greer made love till dawn, like there would never be enough, like "Dontchu know you make me wanna shout!"

Jane let herself dream like she used to before the children, yearn like she usedta before stretch marks and nursing, be who she was when Greer first courted her, a lady of intellect, mystery and surprises. A woman who'd not be taken for granted, or slight herself by forgetting how much she was and could be. Jane made love with a passion Greer had to change his style for. She wanted him to know the difference between wife and Jane, Mommy and Jane, social worker and Jane. Jane was still becoming herself.

TEN

"Greer, how do you have the energy for all this Africanizing every morning?"

Jane looked rather chic in her psychiatric social worker suit, all beige and taupe. She was smiling more than usual too, but Greer went right on, though he was grinning himself up a storm of hellacious rhythm:

"The Negro race is a mighty one
The work of the Negro is never done
Muscle, brains, and courage galore

Negroes in this house
Meet me at the back door!"

On and on he went almost dancing, pulling Jane into poses quite inappropriate for her attire. He wanted her like last night or this morning, all undone. Yet he kept a drumming and the children kept a coming, one after the other, half-dressed, heads uncombed, pieces of homework to be checked in their hands.

"Daddy, what's the matter with you. We up," Betsey half-whispered, wiping sleep from her eyes. Charlie'd started to put the trash out. How in the hell did he know what was on Uncle Greer's mind? Margot and Sharon were trying to do each other's hair. Allard was in the garage lighting matches. One apiece for the KKK. "That's a way," he'd say. "Burn em away, God, burn em away." Vida smelled the fires and gave Allard a running chance to miss that switch she'd pulled to snap some sense into his brain, but Greer was just a drumming and a dancing in the kitchen like nobody had to go to work or to school.

"All right, Uncle Greer, let's start the morning quiz. I got a bus to catch."

"Yeah, Daddy, we got to go all over to the white folks' part of town and that aint no little bit of way, either." The children chimed in one upon the next.

"There's no quiz this morning," Greer said matter-of-factly and stopped drumming. "Actually this is more important than a morning quiz. The time has come for us to do something about our second-class citizenship, and this separate but equal travesty we call our lives. This Saturday we are all going to demonstrate at that racist paragon of southern gentility, the Chase Hotel.

Jane couldn't believe her ears. After everything they'd been through with Betsey, last night, how could he imagine that her children were going to confront wild dogs, hoses, redneck cops, and foolish peckerwoods throwing bottles, eggs, tomatoes, whatever their trashy little hands could find, on her children? Not in this lifetime.

"Greer Brown, you can take your black ass down to the Chase and let them rough you up, but not one of my children is stepping out this door!"

"They're going. It's their struggle."

"You going to risk my children's lives to pee after some po white trash, or rich white trash for that matter. You are a fool, if you think I'm goin to let you get away with that! You are out of your mind! If you think Brown vs. Ferguson was something, you wait till you hear the doings of Jane Brown vs. Dr. Greer Brown. I mean it! Not one of my children is going to any demonstration. You want a wife and family or you want the colored to drink water all round town, anywhere they want to drink water? You get one or the other, Greer Brown: me and my children or you and the race. It's as simple as that."

"Usedta be a body could find a Negro boarding house, Greer, where the colored could be themselves and not worry bout trash and they doings and carrying on," Vida interceded as gently as possible before she went outside to her dahlias.

"That's not enough. Either we're citizens or we might as well be slaves."

At this point Jane made a motion with her arm for the children to get on to their buses, to get out of her sight before all hell broke loose.

"Greer, I always knew there was a fool somewhere deep down inside of you, but I never in my life imagined that you thought you could use my children to fight a colored folks' battle that colored *men* haven't won yet! You are either crazy or beside yourself with fever."

"Jane, this is a matter of integrity."

"Integrity, my ass! It's a matter of my babies' lives!"

"That's why we're going. For their very lives."

"You can take your foolish behind anywhere you goddam well please, but not my babies."

"Who am I, Jane?"

"What are you talking about who are you? You're my husband."

"What does that mean, Jane?"

"Right this minute I can't tell you what the hell it means!"

"It means the children are going to participate in the struggle of their people, your people too, by the way. And they're going to do it cause I said so. I'm the man in this house."

"You definitely are a jackass. I can't say what kind of man you are, but if you're going to play God with my children that I labored with, that I birthed, you best recall how to do all of it, cause I'm leaving your black behind right here, with the race, the children, the bills, the dishes, the fights, the homework, the tears, and everything those children are every day, while you so high and mighty at the Negro hospital. Why don't you go over *there* and demonstrate? Say don't let the Negro people live, let em die till we can get em in the white folks' hospital. Let em die of thirst till they can drink white folks' water. Let em die. Greer, how can you risk our babies?"

"I thought you'd know the answer to that. 'And a little child shall lead them.'"

Jane sat at the kitchen table stiff, though her cheeks were quivering. Greer had always had it in him to be that kind of man, but she never thought she would see the day when he went back on their marriage vows, "to love and honor." She didn't believe this was happening to her.

"Greer, are you telling me that no matter what I say or do, you are taking my children to God only knows what on Saturday afternoon for the sake of the colored who don't even know where the Chase Hotel is? You're going to let my babies face battalions of police and crowds of crackers? Greer, they're children."

Greer poured Jane a cup of coffee just how she liked it: cream first, coffee, two sugars.

"We're going. We're all the ammunition we've got."

"I'll leave you, Greer. My babies aren't cannon fodder. I may be your wife, but I don't have to watch you feed my babies to crackers on a silver platter. 'Here, come and get em, they're not even full grown.'"

"We're going. Jane, why don't you come with us?"

"Cause my life is worth more to me than peeing after white folks!"

"I love you. I'm doing this for you. I'm doing what a man's supposed to do for his wife and children, Jane. Can't you see that?"

"I see my babies aren't safe. I see you ruining a marriage that's already been through hell and survived. I see you throwing away all we worked for. Greer, anything but my babies! I'll go, but please don't take the children. Please, Greer?"

Jane tried to rise from her seat, but her knees were weak. Greer caught her in his arms. "I love you. This is your home. I'm your husband. Nothing's going to change that."

"No, Greer. I can't be here with you to see my children mangled. I don't know right now if I can be with you at all. Mama will stay here while I, uh, go do something somewhere."

Greer tried to hold her close to him but she pulled away. "I know you're my husband and I can't do anything about that right now, but I won't share this savagery with you. I . . . I will let you know, if I'm coming back. Just tell the children Mommy went away for a while. That's all you're to say."

Jane inched slowly out of Greer's arms and went to pack some things. She didn't know where she was going. She didn't know if she was doing the right thing. She knew she couldn't watch what might happen to her children. The race needed something, but not with her babies. Greer was right about integrity, but not with the babies. She was stonelike and rigid, laying the photos of each one of them on her nightclothes in the suitcase. She felt ashamed, but she had to go.

Greer felt the front door slam all the way in the kitchen. He sat down praying she'd understand and come back. He needed her, more than ever. He was taking his babies to a battle he wasn't sure he'd win. He was leading his children of his own free will to face what grown Negroes had already died for. He'd die for Jane, for any of them, but she didn't understand that yet. Greer prayed his kind of prayer for the spirits of the Lord, somebody to bring his wife back. She was such a good woman. Just the woman he'd needed all his life. She didn't know where she was going, but he didn't know how to go on without her.

Oh, he took the children to the demonstration all right. But nobody was hurt. The police didn't even knock any heads. Greer had no way to tell Jane all the children were safe. He didn't know where she was. He didn't know if she was coming back, but he'd done what he had to. A man had to stand for something.

Betsey was doing Margot's hair who was doing Sharon's hair who was tying Allard's shoelaces.

"Listen y'all," he said, "Mama went away for a while and that's all he said."

Betsey tried her best to reassure the children that Jane was coming home, but she didn't know any more than her father had told her. "She gone away for a while."

"Well, where's Mommy?" Allard whined continually.

"We could help Grandma and cook and tidy," Sharon added. "Least till Mama gets back."

"Aunt Jane always kept cookies in the pantry. Uncle Greer doesn't know how to run a house," Charlie grumbled.

"I wisht she was home," Sharon cried over Allard's shoes.

"I want Mommy," Allard screamed.

"Hush up, you hear! You gonna make Grandma get agitation of the heart. We'll be all right. You'll see."

Greer didn't wake them with the conga drum anymore. He didn't even give morning quizzes. He just patted the children's hair into little humps that looked like dunce's caps, gave them too much money for lunch, and went off to the hospital. He tried watching sports with them, boxing, baseball, but there was someone missing.

"When is Mama coming back?" Allard pouted.

Vida did the best she could, but she missed her daughter, and keeping up with all these children was really more than she could handle. It was hard for her to sleep at night, listening to all the children praying for their mommy.

"Grandma, I want my mommy, I want my mommy." Then Vida would carry little Allard to sleep with her.

ELEVEN

Betsey prayed more than anyone knew for her mama to come back to her. But when Carrie came she figured everything would be all right.

Now Carrie was a big woman, bigger than anyone on Vida's side of the family or Greer's. Even Aunt Marie, who talked in tongues and ran a farm all by herself, couldn't have been as big as Carrie. And Carrie straightened her hair so funny. It made her look even bigger. Cause she didn't curl it, she just ran a hot comb through it, so it pointed out in all directions like a white man's crew cut. And she had pierced ears like Aunt

Mamie's, who was ninety. The ears like to touch her shoulders, they were so long and narrow. But more than all of that, Carrie wore two housedresses at the same time, one on top of the other. One up till lunch then the other till she went up to her rooms on the top floor, where the white folks who lived there before left all this junk, scrapbooks and crinolines and things.

Carrie tied her dresses with a rope, a real thick rope. Not like one for hanging clothes, but more like one for making a swing on a tree. She always wore it, even when she changed housedresses. And Carrie wouldn't use any of the bathrooms, even though there ought to have been enough for her, cause there was one on each floor. But Carrie said she liked to use the latrine in the cellar cause that's what her mama had in Arkansas. And that's where she went, where she could think about her mama. Which is what every child in that house was doing, thinking bout their mama, when was she coming back, if she was.

Then, Carrie would say, "This here is just a lil bit of independence time. Yo' mama's coming back for sure. Who could leave a passel of younguns like y'all. Not a soul, 'lieve me, not a livin soul. Allard, put them matches down."

Vida was very quiet, tending her dahlias: each petal was her Jane. Who could tell what could happen with a ruffian like this mindin the chirren. Her beautiful dahlias.

What bothered Vida was that Carrie was never in a particular hurry to do anythin. Not that the laundry wasn't air-fresh clean, and the chandeliers were sparkling, as was the silver. It wasn't that the children didn't get their meals. Vida just couldn't figure out when Carrie did it. Was something natural to it and Carrie wasn't working at all. Plus, Carrie kept visitors, or rather a visitor, Mr. Jeff, who was planting more geraniums than the Browns' backyard had ever known.

Everybody knew about Carrie and Mr. Jeff. That was called a "scandal" according to Margot. It was funny to Allard cause Mr. Jeff was so handsome and Carrie was peculiar to his mind. Allard always teased, "Mr. Jeff's come a courtin." Carrie'd shake her finger at him and say, "Hush you' mouth. Mr. Jeff and I are jus' pals. Aint that right Mr. Jeff? We ju' close friends," squeezing his hand.

Mr. Jeff was the perfect gardener and the spiffiest dressing one you could lay your eyes on. The children didn't understand what a polished-up fellow like Mr. Jeff would want with Carrie, that heavy-set sprawl of a woman, with her hair sticking every which way, when the MacKenzies had that cute little Puerto Rican, Maria, tending children, and the Jacobs a nubile Mississippian watchin after the infant twins. But Mr. Jeff proceeded.

"I'm a gardener and my partners are the ladies with the chirren. I sho' do like to grow things: episia cleopatra, lilacs, cactus, and geraniums of course." With an orange carnation in hand, he sidled up to Carrie asking if she liked tiger lilies, too.

Carrie looked all about herself to see where she was gonna put these flowers on her. While she patted herself, trying to find the right location, Mr. Jeff took her by the hand to the granite bench near the fish pond, lifted the flowers from Carrie's hand, tossin one flower to the fishes and the other tween her bosoms like a fragrant kiss.

"I sho' do like to grow things, Miss Carrie. Are you free on Mondays, Tuesdays, Thursday, even Sunday, M'am? I know I takin some liberties, but there's just something about you that entices me."

Carrie leaned way back to scrutinize this scalawag come-a-courtin in broad daylight with the children all about.

"Grandma, Grandma was sick in bed
Called the doctor and the doctor said
Grandma, Grandma you aint sick
All you need is a lickin stick."

Sharon and Margot chanted behind the bushes. Charlie and Eugene dunked baskets, impressing each other, letting Allard dribble the ball, while Betsey read Countee Cullen poems she'd dug out of her mother's things. Betsey was reading Countee Cullen along with Eugene's arms: sinews. Something about sinews that made poetry more rousing than she remembered.

Then, there was Mr. Jeff, lifting a silver decanter of blackberry brandy in fronta Carrie's nose and toward her lips. After much southern twisting of the shoulder and coy, Carrie sipped a swig or two. It was good Vida was in the front. She never even thought a man would look at Carrie, and that had soothed her soul. What man would want a woman like that hooligan from the swamps or the hills or wherever she came from? It was good Vida couldn't see Betsey gettin a kiss for every long shot Eugene successfully made. And Carrie gettin a snuggle for every promised Thursday and Friday or any ol day just come on round, the chirren just bout take care of theyselves.

Sharon and Margot leapt into double-dutch with the MacKenzie girls: 10, 20, 30, 40, 50, 60, 70, 80, 91speed em up, gotcha mama, but when Mr. Jeff took a holdt to Carrie's thigh, almost all the children burst into a chorus, "Jeff's come a courtin, Jeff's come a courtin." All this is cept Eugene and Betsey, who were busy kissin behind the garage. Eugene was looking for some of the same things Mr. Jeff was looking for, but Betsey didn't know and Carrie wouldn't have it.

"Jeff's come a courtin, Jeff's come a courtin."

Mr. Jeff looked at Carrie as if to say, I thought you could handle these younguns, but maybe not.

"Scat now, chirren. Do like I say, I gotta mess of porkchops with rice and gravy just longing to go to waste, if I don't get my way. Scat now. For your own sake, you bettah do what I say."

The girls disappeared to some far reaches of the yard to eat honeysuckles. Eugene and Betsey liketa set Allard himself on fire when he found them squinched up behind the garage back wall. Of course, he lit a match to say, "I'ma tell! I'ma tell! Betsey's not a good girl and she's goin to Hell."

"Allard, you get outta here! You hear me! I'll slap you good, if you tell on me," Betsey screamed. Eugene's tongue caught Betsey by surprise, but what a kiss. Her eyes clouded over. The smoke she felt must be Eugene's kissing, but it was Allard killing off Nazi warplanes with a pile of newspapers. Eugene ran for the hose.

Betsey took the time to straighten herself up. But she didn't want to, not really. There were two kinds of flames. Both of them dangerous, if they got out of control. Eugene lifted Allard by the seat of his pants and swatted him a good one.

"I'ma tell. I'ma tell y'all was kissing. I'ma tell Daddy, and Grandma and Mommy too."

"Whatchu gonna tell an to who? I swear for Jesus I smell smoke round heah." Carrie huffed behind Allard's left shoulder.

There was smoke everywhere. Eugene and Betsey scrambled by, but Carrie caught Betsey by the arm.

"You stay right heah with me, gal. You and me gotta lotta talkin to do. And you, Boyd boy, you get on too. All I've gotta do is have a fine afternoon with Mr. Jeff and y'all gonna act the fool."

Betsey could smell the blackberry rum on Carrie's breath and noticed she'd changed her morning dress to the evening dress, still with the rope, mind now, yet much more elaborate. Mr. Jeff was waving a kiss down the driveway and Carrie moved her flowers to her hair and behind her ears.

"What do you think Dr. Brown's going to do with me, if he finds the garage burnt up, or Betsey in some rarefied trouble? Y'all aint got no home trainin, no sense of style. There's ways to do things and ways you caint. Y'all simply sufferin from malnutrition of manners. All hugged up on a garage door, in your school clothes at that! Didn't have time to put your poem book down, so busy with that Boyd boy's eyes. Allard, I told you WW II was over, but WW III gonna start tween you and me, if I so much as hear you gotta flame near you or anybody else. Yo' behind's gonna be on fire. You can believe that.

"Now everybody go on and pretty up for dinner. Dr. Brown likes you lookin' neat and clean when he comes through the door. He's been feeling mighty low since, well you know, since your mama's been gone. So don't nobody be putting on no show of niggerness. And Betsey, don't you be doin' every little thing that Eugene tells ya. You and me gotta heap of talkin to do, a heap of talkin, I'd say. Sharon and Margot, take them nasty plants out yo' mouth. Come, get ready for dinner. Y'all just suffer so from malnutrition of your manners, and comin from a good family, too. If I'm holding company, don't y'all come mess with me. There's many a fool who got on my wrong side and never got up to get on the right side."

Carrie buzzed and mumbled all the way to the back stairs where she could see Mr. Jeff was lingering for a sweet good-bye. How could she do it with Vida coming up the way? She beckoned him to the back, but he insisted on the near side porch. And sure enough Vida came strolling by to see the whole of it.

"Mr. Jeff, aren't you workin a bit late this evening?"

"Why yes, M'am, Mrs. Murray. Those geraniums been givin me the dickens these days."

"I can't imagine why a geranium or two could hold you as long as twilight, but I guess there's some things I'll never understand." Vida raised her eyebrows in Carrie's direction. "I'll never understand some things."

"Mrs. Murray, dinner's bout ready." Carrie smiled.

"Bout time, I'd say." Vida retreated to the parlor. Jeff and Carrie stole a bit more brandy and some refined country loving in the doorwell at the side porch.

Carrie wasn't worried bout anything. She had these chirren under control. Set the table just like that. Simmer, don't boil the potatoes. Lift the chicken and porkchops ever so lightly and lay em on a napkin so the oil seeps right on out. Comb your hair. Wash your hands. We're gonna make this house be as grand as we want it to be. It aint white folks what set the style of manners nohow. It was a colored left to do the prettiness round them tables.

Mr. Jeff had fallen for Carrie, not cause of her looks, but on account of her sense of style. She brought some color to his garden and some wildness to his heart. Sweet brandy. Loose honey.

"Carrie, everything's ready," Betsey screamed out the back door. Sweet young thing. Sweet brandy had a lot to learn.

"I'm comin, honey. Watch now, don't let anything overcook."

Betsey looked at the table set ever so delicately. She and Carrie had decided to make everything wonderful for her father, since Jane had gone, but Betsey couldn't bear to look at the empty chair at the other end of the table from her father, so she hid it in her room where she sat at night wishing her mother back.

In her mother's chair Betsey enjoyed memories she thought were only hers, like the time they'd fallen out the canoe at Kentucky Lakes and swam like fishes insteada catching them. Or the nights Jane dressed up in white satin and asked Betsey to do the rear snaps. The special nights Jane read Shakespeare's sonnets or Langston Hughes to the whole passel gathered at the foot of her bed. Then it was time to clean teeth and scatter through the halls to the bedrooms till morning. Betsey thought on her mother's running away, like she'd run away to get something she didn't have. But what it was that the children and Greer couldn't offer Jane was beyond Betsey's comprehension. Betsey'd cry sometimes, or dress up like her mother, parade by the mirrors, checking herself as Jane had for a hanging slip or a chipped nail. Now, that was the way to behave like a lady: nothing out of order and smelling delicious.

"Betsey, c'mon down for your supper," Carrie whispered in the child's ear. "Your mama's gonna come on back heah directly. Don't you be frettin bout that. She'll be back."

With that Carrie rubbed Betsey's shoulders, loosening them a bit. A child shouldn't be so nervous to Carrie's mind, and Carrie'd had six of her own, so she should know a lot about boys and girls, men and women, loss and treasure.

"Carrie, did you love your mother more than anything?" Betsey asked hesitantly.

"Why yes, I did, chile. Far as I was concerned the sun rose and set on my mama. She was the most beautiful woman in the world. She worked so hard and loved us so much, even them lickings we got never changed my mind bout my mama. Mamas only do things cause they love you so much. They can't help it. It's flesh to flesh, blood to blood. No matter how old you get, how grown and on your own, your mama always loves you like a newborn. Yeah. I love my mama even though she's dead and gone. I think on her sometimes. Then I think on my own chirren all round the world, whether they know I love them all, even though they seemed to have forgotten bout me." Carrie's face softened for a moment.

"But Carrie, I don't think children ever forget their mothers. I'm sure your children haven't forgotten about you. I wouldn't, Carrie. I won't ever forget about you, or my real mother."

Carrie hugged Betsey and led her to the dinner table, where they said grace the way Jane did and asked that Jesus bless her.

Carrie had established a routine for after meals. Margot and Sharon cleared the table. Betsey or Charlie washed the dishes and stove. Everybody helped take the trash outside, on accounta really big waterbugs and roaches that loved crumbs. Carrie swept the floors and saw to it everybody had room to do their homework, while Vida crocheted by the veranda watching the sun go down, or the moon rise.

Something had definitely come over the children. Vida wasn't sure if she liked it or not. Things went so smoothly, even on Carrie's day off, that Vida's heart condition was alleviated. Vida could take strolls up the street to visit her only real friends, the Williams sisters, who were also up in age. These strolls reminded Vida of her Frank and her youth. She wondered if Frank would have liked St. Louis at all. Did he see her marching about the world, and their children all grown up and married?

When Vida disappeared on one of her sojourns, Carrie'd give lessons on what a good Negro woman was supposed to know if she wanted a good Negro man. It was appalling to her when she realized that not one of the girls knew what a good Negro man appreciated most in his ever-loving heart: a finely pressed dress shirt. Simple as that.

"Do you know how to cook?"

"No." The girls looked askance.

"Well, can you sew?"

"No, of course not," was their retort.

"It must be you can iron," Carrie proclaimed.

"No," they giggled back.

"It's not that you don't look good and got fine features, and you got no criminal charges against you, but how do you expect to catch a fine young man if all you can do is look nice most of the time? A skillful hand and a pretty face is what you want to present to a man with good taste. You've got the genes and your health, but you've got to know how to iron, or at least how to starch clothes."

The girls said nothing.

"Caint starch clothes, either, huh? Well we've got our tasks laid before us."

With that Carrie gave detailed explanations of how to starch and iron ruffles. How to sew a seam and peel a potato as close as possible. She was going to see to it that these girls were educated in the common everyday things of life.

Now it wasn't like Betsey didn't singe a few things, and Margot and Sharon weren't quite gifted needleworkers, but there was an inkling of reality in their lives now. These children always playing make-believe in their mother's bedroom with negligees, high heels, feathered hats. There was more to being a woman than that. Carrie knew these things. A Negro man wanted a clean shirt, dinner on the table, and some quiet round the house.

Before Carrie came, the children would answer the phone shouting: "Mama, it's a white man" or "Daddy, it's somebody colored." Now they all knew to say "Good Afternoon, Brown Residence," or "Good Evening, Brown Residence." Carrie would have no shenanigans with her brood. She figured there were enough hoodlums in the world already and she was gonna do her best to make sure her charges didn't join them.

She kept everybody busy polishing the stairwells, removing little bits of dust from corners nobody would ever see, turning the blinds at midday so the furniture wouldn't show sun-streaks. When all that was done they could go and play, but not before the house was just perfect. Carrie wanted Mrs. Brown to be pleased when she returned. Carrie had a spirit-feeling that Mrs. Brown wasn't gonna be gone for too much longer. Dr. Brown was too good a man to run off on and a good man was hard to find.

Now that the Boyd boy was hanging around all the time, Carrie was sure she'd have her hands full trying to explain some important facts to Miss Betsey Brown. Carrie'd had six children of her own and Betsey was getting to that stage where a girl's body is way ahead of her brain.

TWELVE

Vida prayed for Jane's return every day. She couldn't imagine her daughter had run off crazy mad. Just up and gone. Forcing that Greer to find this strange woman, Carrie, to take over the chirren, when she could have done it by herself, even with a bad heart. Vida's trips around the house were not merely walks. She was keeping her eyes out, poking around and spying on Carrie.

"She works roots. I'm sure of it," whispered Vida from the rocking chair on the front porch. She goes out on the town. Roots and goes out on the town with that silly rope dangling from her waist. Good Jesus, give me some peace. I know she's got some honey by her bed, persimmon by her head. I can feel it in my bones. Bet you she's got blueing underneath the toilet. She talks low-down and acts the same.

Vida pulled herself from the rocking chair to go look for her fan. It was getting much too quiet. She was usedta the noise of the chirren who no longer made that kinda noise. Carrie had them under a spell. Since she'd come they acted as if they respected each other, and grown folks, too. Vida went looking for her fan, she needed a breeze, something to calm her nerves. It was just too much to share the same roof with a woman like that. Why, ever since she'd come, the chirren acted as if they had some sense. Her fan was around there somewhere. She'd climb the back stairs cautiously. Come down the front stairs regally. No fan. No drawings on the wall. No dust. No cobwebs hanging from the ceilings. "Huh hum hum, what's become of the colored race?" Then Vida would go take her afternoon nap, praying in her sleep for Jesus to solve the mystery of this Carrie woman. Get her out of the house and bring Jane back.

While the children were away at school, Carrie had plenty of time to tend to the preparation of dinner or the small needs of Mr. Jeff. Mr. Jeff stopped by afternoons with sprigs of fresh mint and a couple of flowers from the other yards he kept so exquisitely. A touch of something special and a round of southern whiskey. Now, Carrie wasn't swept off her feet. She liked to entertain and have some company. In a house that soon to be fulla children, a moment of quiet adult conversation was a treasure, Jeff and Carrie found so little time to hold company; either the children would come bouncing through the garden and the porches, or Vida would be stirred from her afternoon nap, which was always calamitous.

Vida would peer through the screen door or come right up to them, saying: "Why, Mr. Jeff. Why are you botherin yourself with the flowers in this garden. Carrie'd been so careful with all the blossoms and other things, she surely must have mentioned. And indeed, we have no plans to hire a gardener who comes by more than once every two weeks."

Mr. Jeff rose slowly, slipping the flask of hard liquor to Carrie.

"Oh no, M'am, I'm sure I so overbooked, I couldn't possibly add another home to my list of bookings. Yes, I am a fully booked man. I stopped by here on accounta Carrie told me there was some malodorous growths by your back fence. I came to dig them up before they spread, and to check the grounds to make sure they won't spread. That's all."

"Why, you know, Missus, there's some mint I came across way out back by the fence. In Arkansas we make a batch of sweet mint tea, specially when there's this kinda heat. Then we mix it with the smallest drop of southern bourbon, just for fighting off the chill."

Vida was still suspecting something else to be revealed.

"Mr. Jeff, is that thing Carrie holdin in her hand some mint, or some other kinda root."

"Oh that's definitely mint. Yerba buena by it's proper appellation, I do believe."

"Well," said Carrie, "I think we might as well share a bit of southern delight with his home grown, how do you call it, Mr. Jeff?"

"Yerba buena."

"Yes, with this heah yerba bueno. I'll run on to the house and make up a good ol' pot of tea, laced with just the tiniest drop of southern whiskey. That ought to help you out with your heart, Missus. Calm your nerves and all, relax your whole system. I'm gointa check on the chirren, though I caint say I heah em. They might be into mischief, though I doubt it. They must be doing their chores, bout now. I'll be coming on back. Don't you worry none."

Carrie ambled to the kitchen with a small smile on her face.

Vida chirped away to Mr. Jeff, "She has really got to go. She's workin roots, Mr. Jeff, don't you think? The chirren are under some terrible spell. They're all so quiet. I swear, she gotta go. There's something hellish bout this rapid downright civilized behavior. It's absolute hellbent."

"No, M'am, I think it's opposite of what you say. I think the chirren are growin up, that's all." Jeff took a flower from his little bouquet and handed it to Vida. "I'll be coming back shortly to check the rest of the yard for fungus and such."

"Why thank you, Mr. Jeff, but keep an eye out for Carrie's meanderin round the garden. See if she hasn't planted some things unbeknowst to you. I'm goin in the kitchen to see after supper. Can't be too careful. With chirren, I mean." Vida sighed.

Vida entered the kitchen slowly like the simmering of greens and porkchops was escaping. She saw Carrie straighten up to say hello, but paid it no mind. Vida announced to all the children gathered in a circle around Carrie, "I'm going to have to speak to Carrie alone for just a minute, chirren. Why don't you go outside and play?"

"Right now, Grandma," Margot responded, her eyes big and bout to tear.

"Are you going to say Carrie caint stay with us anymore?" an alarmed Betsey asked.

"No, chirren, don't you worry bout anything like that. I am just going to have a few words with Carrie, that's all. Now will you all excuse us for just a few minutes."

Vida stood quite calmly in the midst of all her grandchildren running for the back yard. All except Betsey, who hid on the back steps, listening.

"Now Carrie, what you do on your days off is your very own private business, but entertainin gentlemen callers when you're 'sposed to be lookin after my grandchildren is not acceptable behavior. Now if you want Mr. Jeff to come callin, you'll have to do it when you're not here. If I catch you again, I'll have to tell Dr. Brown. And you know he won't stand for any foolishness around his chirren."

Vida felt she'd been very fair, more than fair. She could have not consulted with Carrie at all and just waited for Greer, to tell him all about the whiskey and Mr. Jeff lingerin in the back bushes like a snake. Yet that's not what she'd done. Vida patted her heart and thought on her Frank, who was the last one to give her flowers so long ago. The melody of her romance waltzed through her soul: *Frank and I would get together, when the music got ta playin . . . once I went to a roadhouse and danced on a dime . . . me and that handsome Frank of mine.*

Betsey watched Vida flow up the stairs as if she'd been transformed from a vengeful witch to the good fairy. Betsey crept into the kitchen, ran to hug Carrie, who patted her head and soothed her young charge's fear.

"No chile, I aint goin nowhere. Don't you worry bout a thing. I'm gointa stay right here with you. I've made enough mistakes in my life awready. That's why I came to St. Louis, to find someplace clear of my past with all those mistakes."

"You made a mistake, Carrie?"

"Yeah," Carrie answered, turning back to the stove filled with pots justa bubbling. "Not just one, either."

Charlie came in the door in time to hear the last of Carrie's remarks. "I don't believe it."

"Me either," a panting Allard added.

"Well, you can take me at my word or be fandangled till the day you die, but good and perfect is not what living is about. I know y'all wanta think the best of me, but I've been thru plenty of mess in my days. And I pray to a benevolent God that I'm reformed and moved on to a better way."

"But Carrie, I know you didn't ever do anything that was really bad," Betsey retorted.

Carrie reached underneath her apron to pull out some worn photographs stuffed in little plastic pockets.

"These heah are my chirren. They could tell you what was wrong with me. Evil, triflin and simple minded is what I was. I had me four husbands, each one more low down than the last. See this here was my youngest. Rather than stay with me he hightailed it for Korea. Don't know his whereabouts now. My baby. This picture's all I've got of him. Oh, heah's my daughter. She's still alive up in Chicago. She dances. That's why she don't have on too many clothes. I heah she really somethin to see, flashin by some white men, who give her flowers and whatnots to remember them by. See, look at all the white men by her side. She sent me this a few years ago. Then somethin happened and I didn't heah from her no more. But she awright, I guess."

Betsey looked at the worn photographs, tryin to see a resemblance of Carrie in each one of them, but they all looked different. Like they weren't from the same family. Yet Carrie was oblivious to the puzzled looks on the children's faces.

"Oh, this one here in his uniform, that's my middle son. Gone and married some German woman over there and got me a grandson, or so they say."

Carrie continued her peculiar teachings and quirks, while the children brought home tales of the ways of white folks and young love. Vida managed a thin acceptance of the woman whose hair stood on edge like there'd been a short in the electricity somewhere.

Polishing crystal was one of Carrie's more enjoyable tasks. She liked to run her fingers long the rims and have tinklings ending as she began another. A luxurious hum to her mind. Wine glasses, cognac glasses, water glasses, liqueur glasses melodiously helping her pass the day.

Vida bided her time on the upstairs porch thinking on her Frank. How they used to play, running after each other behind the road houses near Charleston. The time Frank went all the way to Atlanta only to come back and say he'd seen some gal from the bottoms working in a house of ill repute, and that he'd prayed for her and convinced her to lead a good Christian life. Vida thought that was so admirable. It never occurred to her to ask what it was that Frank was doing in that house of ill repute in the first place. Oh, but when that music got to playing, she and Frank would get to swaying, and all that was on Vida's mind was her memories and the smell of salt air at dusk. Greer had been nice enough to put a canopy with mosquito nets over her bed, as well as finding a mauve chaise longue which he said was good for her back. Vida counted her lace handkerchiefs, fingered her daguerreotypes and sang love songs to her buddy who was waiting on her for sure.

It was a lovely day to do anything in the city of St. Louis. To go down by the river and look at East St. Louis where all them gaming houses and hoodlums were, or to jump on the back of a trolley and ride all the way downtown without being caught. Ordinarily Betsey would have stuffed herself with honey from the honeysuckles that grew wild all about the town, but today she didn't even see the cherry trees in full bloom nor the azaleas creeping out toward the roadway as if they were making a flowering pavement for reigning nobility, or just for Betsey herself. She didn't see any of those things. She was hustling long the streets like a woman bout to kick ass or break somebody's arm just cause she felt like it.

Carrie heard all this door slamming and mumbling coming from the front, so she came out to see what was the matter. Miss Vida never made noise. She was too much the lady. So Carrie knew something was the matter with one of those children, but she couldn't find whoever it was. Going from room to room Carrie looked under tables, behind couches, in the closets and behind the stairs. Not a soul was present.

Yet when Carrie went on about her business, which was fixing dinner, she spied Betsey on the back stairway next to new blossoms in Vida's daffodils, just fuming and weeping all at once.

"Why Betsey, honey. Why ain't you at school? You shouldn't be home at this hour. Tell Carrie what's wrong. Did those crackers call you names or throw you out of the games cause you colored? Tell me now and we'll fix it up."

Carrie hugged Betsey and wiped the furrows from her forehead, saying, "That's the way you get wrinkles, from letting things upset you so."

"I'm never going back to that old school. Never. I mean that too, Carrie. They have to pay me a whole lot of money like one thousand dollars to get me to go back there."

Then the tears began again and Carrie kept swishing them away with her callused tender fingers. Something terrible must have happened for her girl to be in such a state.

"Well, if you don't tell me what happened, it's back to that old school, as you call it, right this very minute. Do you hear me?"

Betsey took a deep breath and relaxed into Carrie's warm hug.

"How could anybody be so dumb and be a teacher, huh, Carrie?"

"Well. I don't actually think I get what you mean, chile."

"What I mean is, why did I have to tell her that Paul Laurence Dunbar was an American?"

"Why I do believe he was a colored man and an American on top of that. You right bout that, Betsey. I could testify on that one."

"But this teacher tried to make me think that being colored meant you couldn't write poems or books or anything. She called him an unacceptable choice. Now she did this only cause she doesn't believe that we're American. See I tried to tell them but nobody listens to me cause it's just another nigger talking out the sides of her mouth."

With that Carrie pulled Betsey close to her bosom but firm, like just before you're going to get a whipping.

"I don't never want to hear you call yourself no nigger to

anybody. What's on those white folks' minds is one thing, but you gotta honor your own self and your people. Calling yourself a nigger means you don't believe in your own self. And how you gonna make me proud of you, if you running around acting like what white folks think of the Negro is true. Naw, Betsey, there aint nothin in the world to make you a nigger, not less you honey up to them crackers and peckerwoods and let em walk all over you."

"Well, what am I supposed to do? She's the teacher, not me. And I said that being colored didn't mean that Paul Laurence Dunbar was less than a man or not American. I'm the student. She the teacher. She's supposed to be teaching me. Don't nobody pay me a cent to teach a living soul, Carrie. I bet she doesn't know who Langston Hughes is, let alone Sterling Brown or Countee Cullen."

Carrie started wiping her hands in her apron. She was a mite quiet for her usual self. Then she said, "Humph, I don't know that I'm familiar with any of those names in particular."

"Oh Carrie, they're poets. Mama said they are as good as Rudyard Kipling or even Shakespeare."

"Oh I'm sure I'm not familiar with all them names."

"Oh, Mama could tell you," Betsey chimed, making a strawberry jelly sandwich for herself. "But it doesn't matter if you know about them or not."

"Why don't it matter? You think it's awright for Carrie to be ignorant and let the white folks learn, huh? Why Betsey, I thought you were my best friend."

Betsey left her sandwich and pop on the sideboard and ran over to Carrie.

"Carrie, oh Carrie, you're not ignorant, and we are best

friends. I tell you everything, I swear. But Carrie, nobody ever insults you."

Betsey stood defiant with her hands on her hips, while her little face pleaded for understanding that something dreadful had happened to her.

"Oh, so that's why you aint in school, cause somebody insulted you?"

Betsey turned her back to Carrie and gathered up what was left of her strawberry sandwich.

"There's such a thing as honor, you know."

"And you call running away being honorable, I take it. You just walked outta your class cause you were insulted."

"I got no reason to be insulted by some po' white trash, and I didn't run. I walked out like a lady. Humph! She didn't even know who Paul Laurence Dunbar was, let alone that he was a full-blooded American."

"Grab a towel, sit yourself down and help me with this crystal. No streaks and no smudges. Shine it up right fine, you hear me?"

"Yes, Carrie." Betsey sat at the kitchen table glaring at the wine glasses her mother was so proud of. Not a streak. Not a smudge could be left anywhere.

Beginning the marinating of the meat for supper, Carrie murmured, "Seems to me a body with some pride could go anywhere."

"No, you don't understand. I'm never going back."

"Suit yourself, but mind what I told you bout these glasses. No cracks."

Betsey took the step stool from the corner where the mops and waxing sponges were hidden from view and gently placed each glass where she imagined her mother would want them. When she'd finished, Carrie gave her a glass of milk and two oatmeal cookies she'd made that morning. Then, sort of lady to lady, or woman to woman, she began a very confidential story.

"Hummm, there's this occasion I recollect from when I was young myself. Now not as young as you are, but still young. I remember havin to straighten out some no good with a terrible mouth. I felt I couldn't leave out less I stood up for myself. Oh, a whole lotta folks was busy laughin at me. The rest of em saying I should mind and be careful. See this lil ol' heifer, she carried a knife."

On the edge of her seat, Betsey blurted, "But Carrie, what did you do?"

"That lil ol' twich of a gal callt me out my name. Trying to say that I didn't come from a upstanding Christian God-fearing home and was a kind a evil mess."

"But what did you do, Carrie?"

"Callt her out. I just couldn't do no less." Carrie slugged the last of her coffee, as if the story'd ended.

"Callt her out?"

Betsey pondered what on earth could that mean. Carrie wasn't ignorant, for sure. She used all these words that Betsey'd never heard of.

"What do you mean you callt her out?"

"What I done was to pick her simple behind off the floor. Now that was the first thing I done. After I'd done all that, I put her right out, right out the door."

"You mean you threw her into the street?"

"Smack dab in the middle of the street, if ya know what I mean."

Then Carrie smiled a wicked nostalgic smile that tickled Betsey's sense of mischief and daring.

"Wow! That's what you did? Humph."

Betsey was totally engrossed with the woman, or the twich of a woman, Carrie'd thrown out onto the street. Now, that was really somethin.

"Yeah, Betsey, that's what you gotta do when somebody say somethin that smarts ya or makes ya feel real bad. You gotta call em out and then they won't do none of that no mo'. Make em know ya get mighty upset, if somebody is fool enough to come round bein hurtful, like that teacher of yours. Now if that t'was me, I go call her out bout these colored poets. Make her take a step back. That's good for white folks all the time, don'tcha know?"

"Me? Fight the teacher?"

"Well, you in the right, aintcha?"

"I don't think I know how, Carrie. I can't fight."

Carrie's heavy bosom was justa rumbling round in her housedress, while she listened to Betsey's descriptions of her very own shortcomings.

"I don't mean like in no boxin ring, darlin, but with them words you be throwing round. Surely you could put that cid-didy old woman down. And then carry your pride out withcha in all them long hallways. Then see, when it comes time for somebody to be messin with ya, they gonna know you just gonna call em out."

"Everybody would know not to mess with me?"

By now Betsey was jumping up and down in space like "Sugar" Ray Robinson or Althea Gibson. Betsey the Champ. Humph. My, my, my.

"Well, sho' aint nobody gonna come looking for trouble,

lessen they a fool awready. But that don't happen if ya don't always stand up for yourself."

There was in the kitchen a silence that bound Betsey and Carrie one to the other like blood kin. Something had been passt down.

Perky Betsey Brown picked up her satchel and most ran out the door, shouting, "It's almost lunch time. I think I'm gonna go on back to school."

"I thought you wasn't never going back to that terrible mess of a school," Carrie said, leaning on the kitchen table like nothing had transpired since Betsey's sudden appearance.

Running backwards out the door, Betsey screamed, "I still got my pride, you know."

Carrie watched Betsey running down the street like she'd been chased by a ball of fire. When she turned from the window, she whispered to herself, "'Speak up Ike, 'spress yo'self.' That's Dunbar, the colored American poet, I guess."

THIRTEEN

Just after midnight, when the spirits roam freely with the moon as their guide, Jane opened the door to her house, her husband, her home. She relaxed gainst the closed door, near to wrenching throbs in her chest, her palms sweating like dew. She was cold. She was hot. The staircase so long and winding. How could she make it to the top of the stairs without rousing her children?

Greer was enough motivation. She thought of his arms, his chest covered with twidly nappy black hairs, his hands stroking her hair from right to left, the moustache across his lips.

Jane climbed those stairs with feline grace, a cunning she'd been unaware of for many years. But this time she had to make certain that this man, this particular colored man, was hers forever and ever. Just let some nurse look sideways at him and whoever that child was would be somebody else by the time Jane was through. No, more than that, Jane wanted Greer to feel how she'd grown. To actually grasp her new understanding of him, what he stood for, for their people, for the children.

Oh, Jane'd come home to stay this time, no matter what the current crisis might be in North Carolina or in her own bedroom. Jane Brown wasn't ever going anywhere without this man whose thoughts so provoked her, made her see anew who she was and who they were.

Greer didn't ask where she'd been and Jane offered no information, but an avalanche of passion swept through St. Louis that night. Thunderbolts. Tremors. Sweet rains dusting thirsty bodies. Jane never opened her eyes. She could see his face every time he touched her.

The secret of Jane's return was not very long-lived. The children scampered this way and that, elated that their momma was home with them. There was so much everybody wanted her to know. Greer promised a grand celebration and lifted Jane off her feet nigh to the ceiling so she could say the party was not just for her homecoming, but for the progress of the race. Everybody cheered.

Vida whispered to Carrie, "I think you ought to be a bit more proper, now my child's back. Ya hear?"

Sharon was busy speaking to Carrie from the other side saying, "No cursing or drinking, neither, now Mommy's home." Margot got the last word in; "Don't mention nothin about Mr. Jeff."

Betsey was hugging her mama while the rest of the brood frolicked bout the living room. "Oh, Mommy, it's not the same as when you were here, but the house sure does run good."

"Don't you mean the house runs well, Betsey?"

"Yeah, Mama, that's exactly what I meant."

There'd be no bad feelings or scolding bout anything this day. Not the Sunday Jane Brown came back to her house. Why, Vida wept like she was the abandoned child insteada the sturdy rock of a woman that she was. She wrapped her thin-skinned tawny arms round her baby and kept murmuring bout her prayers to bring her baby home. Jesus never fails you, never lets you down, she sang.

Sharon and Margot pulled Jane's billowing skirt to brag, "We don't fight in bed no more."

"You mean anymore, don't you?"

"That's right, Mommy, we don't." They giggled all the way back to the kitchen.

"Aunt Jane, Aunt Jane." Charlie leaped as if he were dunking a basketball. "I don't steal things from any store anymore."

Then Allard chimed in, "Mommy, I make up songs like Chuck Berry, insteada burning up everything."

Margot and Sharon came running back with peanut butter and jelly sandwiches oozing from their hands, when they announced, "Oh, Mama, we could sing most good as the Shirelles, really."

Betsey felt things were getting a little out of control, so she quite sedately added, "We sing Christian gospel songs like Paul Robeson, too."

"Yeah," Charlie frowned. "Not like that man at the church Carrie takes us to."

Allard jumped up to shout, "Yeah, the one where we could play the tambourine and getta spirit."

Now it was a Brown family tradition to have "showtime" before a Sunday evening dinner. This one was a very special one, since Jane'd come home. Carrie disappeared into the kitchen to do her job and think on this Jane Brown woman. Meanwhile the children lined up like the Fisk Jubilee Singers singing, "Oh Lord What a Morning." Then Allard careened cross the floor like Chuck Berry roostered, squealing, "Roll Over Beethoven." Margot, Sharon, and Betsey sang "Tonight's the Night" in a routine that would have put the Ronettes to shame. Greer brought out his conga drum and for a change, Jane led the merengue line all over the house. This mad, joyous house that was hers. Even Vida got up to do a sassy little two-step.

Slowly Jane slipped from the carnival mood of her household to think of more serious and practical matters. Carrie, for instance, or the girls reaching puberty with no direction.

"I think you boys, yes Allard, all of you, should go on out to play. We've done quite enough for the Negro race today."

Jane smiled watching these wiry gangly short-haired gremlins running for their basketballs. Boys will be boys she thought to herself, as if she'd ever thought anything else.

That was curious: what had she thought would happen to her household while she was gone. She'd speak to the girls first, then her mother, and finally, that Carrie woman.

Actually, Jane asked Carrie to please retire to her room while she visited with her daughters, even if a certain Mr. Jeff was lingering by the back porch. Oh, Jane was a self-contained woman, but a terribly observant one as well. She got so beside herself she stopped Carrie, who was on her way to her room, to have a short talk.

"Carrie, I realize you are at a disadvantage in this situation, since I myself didn't hire you, but I would like to know who gave you permission to stay the loneliness of one gardener, meaning Mr. Jeff, in the presence of my children. Not to mention the fact that you been taking them to some niggerish church to get the Holy Ghost. We are Presbyterians and that is not something Presbyterians get, the Holy Ghost. Plus, you've got them swishing and swaying, doing those dirty dances like the po' children in the projects. You are turning my children into heathens or hoodlums and I will not stand for either. If I were you, I'd mind my place to hold it more securely. Is that clear to you, Carrie?"

"Yes, M'am. That's plenty clear, Mrs. Brown. I know you and me are hardly the same. But I don't see why you'd begrudge me the excellent company of Mr. Jeff. I didn't come here to be meddlin with the way you want your younguns raised, but you weren't round, Mrs. Brown, so I just did the best I knew how. I'll continue with you long as you know my heart's in the right place. I love these chirren like they was my very own, Mrs. Brown, I swear 'fore God, I do. But I'd like to remind you very respectfully, Mrs. Brown, that I'ma full growed woman, working hard to do my job."

Carrie dropped her head slightly and slowly trudged up the servants' staircase, which was actually just the back staircase, but when Jane was in a mood it was the servants' staircase and Jane was in a mood.

"Girls, girls, sit down and we'll discuss the facts of female life. You're all reaching an age when things start to happen to your bodies and new strange feelings might come from your very souls, no, you'll think they're coming from your very soul, but they are, actually, carnal, no, feelings having to do with, growing up."

Betsey asked abruptly, "Mama, you gonna talk about sex? Is that what you're trying to say?"

"Not exactly, Betsey, not about sex per se, but more about how to be a lady. What's fitting for a young girl who will become a lady eventually. Things like always holding your knees together when you are sitting. Always sit with your back straight and your hands in the shape of a delicate flower, just about there."

Blushing, Jane gestured toward the girls' privates.

"Hold your head high. Never lower your eyes or everyone will know you gave it up. Oh, that's not what I mean. I mean people will think you're fast or something, or not a virgin. Oh, for God's sake just do what I say and before you know it you'll be sashaying down the Champs Elysées with a handsome new husband. A young man who appreciates manners."

The girls exchanged curious looks. "Our manners, Mommy?"

"Yes. Your manners, you see, will attract the nice young men who don't respect girls who come across too easily."

From the position Jane had prescribed, Sharon whined, "But Mommy, this is like sitting in school. I awready know how to do this."

"Mama, when can I wear stockings and high heels? I'm too big now for socks with lace." Jane shook her head no. "But Mama, you're not keeping up with the times. Couldn't we just go to Saks and look at them? Could we? Could we please, Mama?"

"Mommy, it's all right with me, I don't like boys anyway," Margot said quite matter-of-factly.

"Margot, now you sound like you've got a good head on your shoulders."

It was Betsey and Sharon who were giving her trouble.

"Mama, you mean to say we gotta stay with our heads high, knees locked, back straight, alla that, just to get a date?" Betsey couldn't believe it. Sharon was morose. Margot liked the whole idea.

"No, you stay that way to stay out of trouble. Oh, I nearly forgot the most important thing. Girls, come close and listen to what I say. Every month something's going to happen. Now it will be strange at first, but you'll get used to it after a while."

With that, Jane hustled the two youngest up to her bedroom, where they wouldn't be disturbed by the boys who were to know nothing about this. It was a woman's secret, according to Jane.

Betsey had let on to her mother that she was listening to every single word Jane said, but in reality Betsey Brown was peeping out the window watching Eugene Boyd and Charlie play ball. Now Betsey sped past Carrie hovering over the stove, when Carrie said intently, "Betsey Brown, you come right on back in here. There's some things I want to say to you, now your mama's brought the subject up. I need to talk to you."

Eugene was opening the back screen door and all Carrie had to say was, "Eugene Boyd, you take your fresh behind and that basketball right on away from here this very minute. You hear me talkin to you, don'tcha?"

Eugene threw Betsey a kiss she pretended landed just beneath her left eye. She sighed one of those sighs her mama'd been warning her about.

"Now, Betsey, you and the Boyd boy got plenty of time for what got him running over here every afternoon and you chasing round him and the basketball like you a referee or something. Now I want you to know you don't need to sit like a statue if some boy takes a whistle at ya. You just smile and go on. They's no trouble worse than fear. You aint 'sposed to be fraid of men and young boys, but what young beau wants to hear you saying, 'My mama said you only after one thing and my knees are locked, so there.'"

Betsey was laughing cause she knew what a kiss could do by now. She and Eugene had a special place by the roses in the far reaches of the yard where they cuddled and kissed and saw stars in broad daylight. Yeah, Betsey Brown sat there justa laughing. But Carrie went on.

"A kiss or two can undo all that mama talkin. Go on ahead and enjoy bein a girl, but be careful. You'll get your share of hugs and squeezes. Young boys can be as sweet as you can imagine. Just hold off from those no-good niggers with the devil in they eyes. Now that's my advice."

Carrie and Betsey suddenly stopped their conversation. Jane

was coming down the front stairway with Sharon and Margot saying: "That's all you need to know right now."

Sharon jumped two steps to confront her mother. "But how do I get a baby?"

Jane was so exasperated she turned beet red and with a straight face blurted, "Just keep those panties up, you hear?"

FOURTEEN

In the late afternoon Vida took to her room, where she rocked by the window not unlike the limbs of the trees she watched so carefully. This is not where her beloved Frank would have left her, but the quiet sway of the branches offered a solace, a soothing of her soul. No children to run behind, no daughter to assuage, in her own room with the breezes and her rocking chair, Vida let the day slip away and gathered her memories that always left a fleeting smile and a slight blush to her cheeks. There was a music to her daydreams that she sang with the wind.

Humming to herself, Jane brushed her hair by her vanity. She couldn't hold back the smile that kept creeping to her lips. She had impulses to giggle or chuckle incessantly. She'd look at Greer exhausted on their bed, one arm hanging from the mattress, the other reaching out to where she might have been, but wasn't. Regally sweeping strokes of auburn whisked from one side of her face to the other. Jane had had such fun. What a great idea that had been to get home before the children and make Paris come alive in their bedroom. She hadn't let him touch her until she'd managed to find her only true lace negligee, then she'd insisted on champagne and liverwurst. Jane did not like caviar. Plus, they didn't have any. Yet liverwurst and champagne with the last scents of afternoon were all they needed to beguine, begin a reeling and a rocking. Jane slid off the bed twice, once gliding down her back to the carpet, the other time wrestling the sheets from her neck while she balanced herself on her head. Her hair fell like a fan around Greer's fingers. Pulling each other up, the champagne spilled across Jane's thighs. With great unladylike élan Jane sipped the bubbles from the bottle til Greer grabbed it from her and kissed the Mumm's from her lips.

"Why don't we do this more often?" Jane chirped from her seat by the mirror. She'd started trying on jewelry and her naked body. Maybe that would be her next flight of fancy: she'd seduce Greer in the nude with jewelry and perfume. That was a good idea. Greer sighed, seemingly weighed down with unseen boulders and chains. He could barely speak, but he tried his damnedest: "If you'd stayed at home, we could have."

Jane stopped brushing her hair. That was not a good idea.

She didn't want to discuss her vacation, as she called it. "Greer, I'm not going anywhere, really." Jane delicately approached her husband, who was nearly falling off the bed. "I think we can work things out. Greer pulled Jane's mouth to his. Maybe they would never get up.

After school everybody had some chore to do, Carrie'd seen to that.

"Margot, go clean them collards and be sure to pick out all the worms. Allard, get the dust broom and start on the back staircase third floor."

Allard pouted, "All the way down from the third floor, Carrie?"

"Yep, that's what I said."

"Sharon, you go right behind Allard with the wax and get them hard-to-clean lil spaces on the banisters, ya hear? Charlie, you go on upstairs and wash them blinds, then turn em so the furniture don't pale in the sun. Get on now. Betsey, stand on this table and clean them crystals on the chandelier and if any one of em breaks, your behind is gonna be hurtin for mo' than a few days."

The telephone rang and Betsey went to answer it. Carrie, majestic in the center of the kitchen, listened to the chant of the children: "Good Morning, Brown Residence. Good Afternoon, Brown Residence. Good Evening, Brown Residence." Oh how those proper voices warmed her southern soul.

"See now y'all sound like ya got some sense. Sharon, go help Margot starch them clothes and while they hanging outside for a bit of repose, carry that silver on withcha. Get it to shinin the way your mama like it to do. Tarnish aint nothing to take pride in, I'll say that. Get on now, busy your selves fore your folks get home."

Carrie heard Mr. Jeff's regular gait coming up the back porch. She ran her hands through her hair quickly, tugged her apron straight, and gleamed a bit as she let him through the door.

"Why Miss Carrie, I didn't realize you had some free time on your hands. Now isn't that God's way of letting you know you doin the right thing."

With that Mr. Jeff handed Carrie a lovely bouquet of gardenias and azaleas. Carrie set off for one of Mrs. Brown's crystal cases, after pouring a sip of Jack Daniels for herself and her guest, the handsome Mr. Jeff.

"Now, Miss Carrie, it certainly is gracious of you to offer me a spot to drink, but on this very day I've brought you some of my own blackberry wine made up just how my mama usedta do in Mississippi. Would you care for a lil?"

Carrie went to the pantry and found two of Mrs. Brown's wine glasses she swore were from France and irreplaceable, so she and Mr. Jeff could enjoy their visit leisurely, as well as with some style. Mr. Jeff's conversations had mostly to do with the change in the Brown children since she'd come.

"Why they were just hellions fore you got here, Miss Carrie. Couldn't nobody talk to em or make em mind. Once I thought I was gonna give that Charlie from up north a good licking for pulling up all the begonias in the Wilsons' yard. I surely did have an inclination to do harm to that boy. If it wasn't for Dr. Brown, I probably would have. But Dr. Brown's sucha hard-working man and he supports the race. I like that in a man, supporting the race."

"I like that in a man, myself," cooed Carrie, feeling the warmth of the whiskey and the sweet blackberry winding through her limbs. "Oh Mr. Jeff, all they needed was some things to do. To find out about themselves. How hard they could work. And what's more, I let em find out on they own. Everybody got they own way, that's what I say. Now they believe they gettin grown and that's all chirren dream of, bein big, bein in charge, being responsible for they chores and they behavior. Yeah, I'm growin me some chirren with some sense."

While Mr. Jeff and Carrie enjoyed their tête-à-tête, the house was reeling with the children shouting back and forth across rooms and up and down stairways.

"Allard, if you don't dust good, my wax don't work," Sharon coaxed.

"Awright, awright. I'ma come back and do it tomorrow."

"No, you gonna do this today. I gotta do my job right."

The Brown children had made up a song to one of the tunes Allard whistled that went like this:

this is our house/ this is our house
we keep it shinin/ spankin clean
if some white folks ever see it
they'll think they musta done it
but it's us colored kids that run it
this is ours

"Hey, Allard, what you call these streaks on here? Some kinda design?"

"Aw Charlie, it just won't come clean."

"You want me to kick your behind?"

"UMMMMMH, Sharon, you should taste this starch. It's so good."

"Get that mess out of your mouth and in the clothes like you know you should!"

this is our house/   this is our house
we keep it shinin/   spankin clean
we aint workin for no crackers
no rich po' white trash
we doin this in our house
cause we gonna make it last.

"You know what?" Betsey asked anybody. "You know what, the neighborhood aint falling down, not unless I do, cause white folks can't clean nothin right."

"Least not quite like we do," Charlie answered.

"I'm done. I'm done," shrieked Allard. "Somebody wanta race down the street free-handed?"

But the rest of the children were still busy with their chores, singing:

this is our house/   this is our house
keepin it oooh   just so
keepin it oooh   just so
Carrie come see/   Carrie come see
keepin it ooh just so
keepin it ooh just so

Carrie snuggled for a minute with Mr. Jeff while looking at her bouquet she'd better take to her room before Mrs. Brown came. Then she took a tour of the house with everyone except Allard, while they showed their handiwork.

"Y'all done a mighty fine job, yep, a mighty fine job. And we gonna have some chicken and dumplings tonight. Y'all deserve it. A mighty fine job, if I do say so myself."

So when Carrie didn't come one Monday morning Betsey figured she would cover for her. She could have done a good job too, cept that Mama and Grandma kept asking her where was Carrie and wouldn't let her do any of the stuff Carrie had taught her to do, which wasn't the way they did everything. So Betsey shouted back at them and got in a terrible argument about being out of her mind as well as an impudence and not showing any respect for her elders.

Just as Betsey was moving the glasses outta the dishwasher to pour juice for the family, Allard tripped on his shoelaces and all the glasses shattered cross the floor. Vida held her heart.

Everything went haywire. Betsey was sweeping up the glass as fast as she could. Allard was still trying to tie his shoes. Sharon was combing her hair in the kitchen, which everyone knew was low-class in the first place. Margot was making sandwiches like a robot. Charlie was just grabbing things out of the refrigerator. Jane was holding on to the sideboard for dear life itself. Greer was reading the morning paper while drinking his coffee. He only liked Kenyan or Guatemalan coffee with three sugars. He was sucha Latin.

"Lord, Lord, please be careful. I do declare, where's that crazy Carrie?"

"Carrie aint crazy, Grandma, she's just not here yet," Sharon calmly explained.

"Well, it doesn't matter if she's crazy or not, ordinarily, but she must be crazy not to come to work today." Jane's tolerance was getting very very short.

"She's comin, Aunt Jane, don't worry," Charlie assured her.

Vida was hovering over everything.

"Please be careful. All this glass. That wasn't your wedding crystal from Aunt Ethel was it, Jane?"

Sharon and Margot were practicing the new Tina Turner song bout bein a fool in love. That did it. Jane went right out.

"No, Mama, it wasn't the crystal from Aunt Ethel. Girls, stop singing that trash first thing in the morning! Everybody please just be quiet! I can't stand all this noise. Greer, would you please do something?"

At that moment the telephone rang and Greer answered it.

"Jane, darling, it's for you."

Jane tried to calm herself.

"Hello, this is Mrs. Brown, may I help you? . . . Carrie?"

Everyone in the kitchen froze at the mention of Carrie's name.

"Well Carrie, where are you? You're supposed to be here. Where are you?"

Betsey whispered to Sharon that Carrie must be going round the bush to her mother.

Jane looked ill.

"Jail?"

"Jail?" the household uttered in unison.

"Well, why?" Jane went on. "Cause you had to cut a friend of yours?"

"Uh oh." The children grimaced.

"Cause you had to cut a friend of yours!"

"That's not so good," Greer looked up from his paper to

say to whoever might be listening. The children were hushed but disquieted bout this turn of events.

"Carrie, you best come round here, when you get out from down there, and carry all of your mess right out of this house."

The children groaned.

"Oh, nooooo, Mama, please, no."

"Get your last check and pay your last respects to Mr. Jeff and whoever else you've been entertaining in my house. You know good and well I can't have a criminal looking after my children!"

Jane turned from the telephone quite her personable self.

"All right, children, off to school with you."

There was an eerie edge to the voices of the children as they filed by for their morning hugs and kisses. Jane sat down to breakfast with her beloved husband. Vida escaped to her rocking chair and sang "My Buddy," thinking on Frank.

Late afternoon came across sooner than usual or maybe it was the sadness Betsey was experiencing in her every sinew. Carrie must have come while they were at school. When Betsey got home all Carrie's things were gone, but she found some of the rope Carrie usedta tie around her waist by the latrine in the cellar.

Her sisters and the boys didn't even realize what had happened. Their losing Carrie and all.

Betsey never mentioned her feelings to her mama cause then Jane would just remind her that she always picked the most niggerish people in the world to make her friends. And she would list Mavis, Charlotte Ann, and Linda Susan who really was just po' white trash. So Betsey didn't say anything.

Betsey just took Carrie's place in the house. Did everything like she would have done except she did use the regular bathrooms. And Betsey prayed for Carrie the way Carrie'd prayed for the one of her chirren most dead.

Betsey couldn't understand how anybody didn't know Carrie wouldn't hurt nobody less they hurt her a whole lot. Carrie wouldn't have cut nobody, not less they hurt her a whole lot.

Somehow the extra stretch to the thickest limb of her tree by the terrace gave Betsey the breath she needed to settle on other thoughts. The moon was peeking through an orange haze. Basketballs were patting driveways like so many conga drums. There was Eugene lurking in the twitch of an eye. Carrie had said it was okay to have feelings like that. Special feelings that tingle and rush through the body. Wrens hovered by the telephone wires.

Betsey lingered over her city making decisions and discoveries about herself that would change the world. In one way or another, anyone who could hear merengues and basketballs, feel loose and free in a comforting oak, was surely going to have her way.

But Carrie would have said there was nothing dishonorable about being an Ikette, either.